"This baby's lucky to have you for a mom. But children need families. Friends. Uncles."

Jordan smiled, hoping she'd take the hint.

Caitlin didn't say anything—just sat there, peering at him, thinking it all over. Jordan knew she would need time to adapt. He was more than willing to give it to her if it meant she would allow him back into her life.

The rest could wait. They had time.
Please God, give her time to accept me.

He wanted her to trust him. He wanted to be there for her, to share part of the burden. And he wanted to go back to a time when he should have grabbed at the adoration she'd so innocently offered.

Watch for the next book in the
BRIDES OF THE SEASONS
series, available in October.

Books by Lois Richer

Love Inspired

A Will and a Wedding #8
†*Faithfully Yours* #15
†*A Hopeful Heart* #23
†*Sweet Charity* #32
A Home, a Heart, a Husband #50
This Child of Mine #59
*Baby on the Way #73

† Faith, Hope & Charity
*Brides of the Seasons

LOIS RICHER

credits her love of writing to a childhood spent in a Sunday school where the King James version of the Bible was taught. The majesty and clarity of the language in the Old Testament stories allowed her to create pictures in her own mind while growing up in a tiny Canadian prairie village where everyone strove to make ends meet. During her school years, she continued to find great solace in those words and in the church family that supported her in local speech festivals, Christmas concerts and little theater productions. Later, in college, her ability with language stood her in good stead as she majored in linguistics, studied the work of William Shakespeare and participated in a small drama group.

Today Lois lives in another tiny Canadian town with her husband, Barry, and two very vocal sons. And still her belief in a strong, vibrant God who cares more than we know predominates her life. "My writing," she says, "allows me to express just a few of the words God sends bubbling around in my brain. If I convey some of the wonder and amazement I feel when I think of God and His love, I've used my words to good effect."

Baby on the Way
Lois Richer

Published by Steeple Hill Books™

STEEPLE HILL BOOKS

Steeple
Hill™

ISBN 0-373-87073-6

BABY ON THE WAY

Copyright © 1999 by Lois Richer

This edition published by arrangement with Steeple Hill Books.

® and TM are trademarks of Steeple Hill Books, used under license.
Trademarks indicated with ® are registered in the United States Patent
and Trademark Office, the Canadian Trade Marks Office and in other
countries.

Visit us at www.steeplehill.com

Printed in U.S.A.

People are not cast off by the Lord forever. Though He brings grief, He will show compassion, so great is His unfailing love.

—Lamentations 3:31-32

For Robynne Rogers-Healey, Ph.D.
You make me laugh, and cry, shake my head and
nod in agreement, but always, always, I appreciate
what a gold mine of blessing you are to my spirit.
Thanks for being the one I can run to, whine beside,
cry on, tease, giggle over and drink gallons of
coffee with no matter how far away we live or
how many changes God sends into our lives.
You are my friend.
I love you.

Chapter One

"It must be terribly difficult for poor Caitlin without her husband. And her being eight months pregnant." The whispered remark of the nurse carried clearly into the hallway.

Caitlin Andrews lifted her face as she slipped around the side of the receptionist's desk and into the foyer, refusing to acknowledge the commiserating look she knew she'd see on the nurses' faces. Pity was the one emotion she couldn't afford right now. She tugged her coat from the rack and slung it over her shoulders before walking outside.

I'll manage, she decided fiercely, braving the gusting wind. She lifted her chin, allowing the watery afternoon sun to warm her. *I always have.*

Of course pregnancy *would* be infinitely more enjoyable with a husband in the picture. She'd never even considered life as a widow, and certainly not before she'd welcomed her first child into the world. This was *not* part of her plan.

"Unfortunately, my plans don't count for much," Caitlin Andrews acknowledged tiredly, thoroughly out of sorts after an hour spent in the doctor's office where she'd watched the scale move further upward.

She crossed the street and moved toward the nearby coffee shop. Pushing the door open, she breathed in the wonderful aroma of freshly brewed coffee.

"You and I are just going to have to make do with what we've got, Junior." The baby kicked her in the ribs to indicate his feelings in the matter.

"And may I remind you that we've only got each other?"

He thumped again, hard and strong. She smiled at the strength of that jab.

The restaurant was filled with people and Caitlin had to wait a few minutes for a place to sit. Finally a mother and her two small children got up and went outside while the father paid the bill.

A family, whole and complete. The picture emphasized her own lonely state and Caitlin made herself look away.

Just get yourself into the booth. Smile. Take off your coat. Pretend everything's fine. Be strong.

"Hi, sweetie. Still growing I see." The teasing waitress winked and plopped down Caitlin's usual order of a pot of tea and a fat bran muffin.

"Hi, Ruth." Caitlin dipped the tea bag into the water, her voice low and controlled. "You're not going to lecture about eating for two again, are you?"

Caitlin had walked miles along the riverbank and faithfully counted every calorie that passed her lips for the past six months. And for all her efforts she'd just increased another two pounds! That wasn't in the plan, either.

"Weight up? It's only natural when...well, you know!" Ruth held out another bran muffin, her smile wicked.

"That is not funny!" Caitlin looked at the friendly woman. "And you should know that someone in my condition is not to be trifled with."

Ruth's hearty chuckle ignored Caitlin's chiding look.

"Someone in your condition shouldn't be out in this weather," she advised lightly. Her long vivid fingernails tapped the table. "Don't you know there's a storm warning out for tonight? Snow and blowing snow."

"It's only the first of October, Ruth. Winter can't come yet." Caitlin smiled placidly, well used to the vagaries of Minnesota weather. "It's just a threat weathermen use to warn us of what's to come. The sun's still shining."

"If that isn't positive thinking, I don't know what is. Honey, you just keep that chin up. You're going to need it." Shaking her head, Ruth glanced down pityingly. "Drink your tea, Mrs. Andrews. You'll feel better."

"I hate tea." Caitlin made a face at the white china pot. "Coffee is the beverage for any hour of the day or night,'' she informed the older woman, noting the sparkle of amusement in Ruth's laughing eyes.

''I've heard. In fact, I think it was the last time you were here. Unfortunately for you,'' the waitress eyed her protruding stomach, ''Andrews Junior doesn't like the stuff. So you get tea.''

''I know,'' Caitlin said. ''And what Junior wants, Junior gets. This kid is going to be a real tyrant.''

The waitress, a slim, youthful mother of five chuckled and turned away to take another order. Caitlin poured out a cup of the steaming liquid, allowing the fresh clean scent of peppermint to soothe her jangled nerves.

For the umpteenth time that day she wished Michael were here to talk to, to lean against, to hold her. And for the umpteenth time she told herself to get on with her life. Michael wasn't ever going to be there anymore. He was dead. There were only her and the baby now.

''Lyn?''

Caitlin was so engrossed in her thoughts of the past that she jumped in surprise. Only one person used that shortened version of her name.

''Jordan.'' She peered up through her lashes, hoping she was wrong.

Oh no, she groaned. Not now. Not today!

''Caitlin. I thought it was you. Your hair is different.''

Her brother-in-law's voice boomed in that deep bass tone she could have recognized from several blocks away. She knew the sound well, heard it in her dreams sometimes. She'd never been able to forget Jordan.

His curious glance moved from her face to the obvious mound of her stomach. She watched his gold eyes widen in surprise.

"Uh, that is, oh." The craggy face, so unlike Michael's, drooped in shock.

She smiled. "Yes, oh. A master of understatement as usual, Jordan."

Not now, she begged silently to the God she hadn't prayed to since that awful night seven months ago.

Please don't do this to me now. Not while my emotions are doing these ridiculous prenatal flip-flops. Not when I've almost made it through this on my own. Not now, when I'd almost convinced myself that I don't need Michael's family.

She opened her eyes but Jordan was still standing there, gawking at her.

"How are you?" Caitlin couldn't help but ask, despite the lump in her throat. Her question was polite, perfunctory, that of one stranger to another.

He didn't pretend civility. Instead he folded his muscle-honed body onto the bench seat opposite hers. As he leaned forward, his face mere inches from her own, she caught a whiff of his tangy lime-scented aftershave.

"I'm just absolutely fantastic now that I know I'm going to be an uncle, Lyn." His tanned face clenched in a rigid mask, his words icy chips of mockery.

The sting of his glittering eyes ate at her, cutting through her carefully preserved mask of control.

Hadn't it always been that way? Hadn't Jordan always cut right to the heart of things?

"Good grief, Lyn, why didn't you tell me? Or Mom and Dad? Someone!"

She watched as he visibly fought to control his temper and that irritated her.

"You weren't here, remember? And your parents have been away on that trip to Europe for the past three months. Remember?"

Caitlin swallowed. He wasn't buying it. Jordan mad was infinitely worse than Jordan bossy.

"What about before they left? Why couldn't you have told my parents you were expecting Michael's baby then?" A muscle twitched at the corner of his mouth, testament to his anger. "It would have meant the world to them."

"I had to get used to the idea first myself. I wasn't exactly expecting it, you know." She glared at him. "By then they were planning their trip to get away, to try to put Michael's loss behind them. It just wasn't the right time." Caitlin flushed.

He *would* put her in the wrong. It was just like old times, she fumed. Unbidden, Jordan's scathing remarks about her elopement with Michael flew across her brain. *She* should have known better, waited a while, stopped to think.

Caitlin had felt like a helpless ninny then, worried that Jordan would think she was marrying Michael on the rebound from him. Stupidly she'd kept quiet, waited for Michael to take charge of the situation, needing his protection against Jordan's pushiness.

Now she was alone. And *she* was in charge.

"Eventually they will know," she explained, easing her aching back against the seat. "Now that they're back, I'll tell them soon."

She shrugged, striving for nonchalance. Jordan Andrews prided himself on his ability to look inside people. It was a trait most folks didn't expect to find in a man obsessed with the intricacies of high-tech computer systems.

"When?"

"This is my situation to deal with, Jordan. Mine. I'll handle it in my own way."

He watched her. Caitlin knew those assessing, calculating eyes could see clear through to the fear that filled her soul. Fear that he'd see how scared she was, fear that he'd seen how easy it would be to give up her staunch determination to manage her life alone.

"It's still the same old story, isn't it, Lyn? You're determined not to let anyone past those steel bars and into your heart."

"Hardly anything that melodramatic, Jordan." She forced a note of calm reason into her voice. If he couldn't be mature about the past, she would.

"I simply felt there was no need to worry your mother and father ahead of time. I've spoken with them once or twice, of course, but I didn't want to disturb them, especially when they were still mourning Michael."

She flushed under his condemning look, her chin thrust out defiantly. "I never meant to *not* tell them!"

"Yeah, right." The exasperation in his voice

mocked her. "And when is the blessed event? By the looks of you, it can't be long now."

Jordan had always been able to get to her weakest spot without really trying. Just a few well-chosen words and Michael's brother could score a direct hit on her most vulnerable area. Right now that happened to be her shape, or rather, the lack of it.

He was the quintessential male, always right, always in control. Once she'd loved that about him, that calm assuredness, that certainty, as if he knew exactly what he was doing with his life. Once she'd thought Jordan would be the man she would marry.

Once she'd been stupid, childish, trusting and he'd pushed her away like an annoying pest.

Well, she wasn't buying into his world again. She was an adult now, in charge of her own life. Not some insecure young girl to be manipulated by the crazy dreams and impossible wishes she'd held ten years ago.

Caitlin couldn't afford to live in make-believe any more. Happily ever after was a nice dream, but it wasn't very realistic. Not for her. She'd figured that out after Michael died.

She reined in her fluctuating emotions with an effort, trying to remember her positive self-talk. It would be a relief if she could vent this building frustration, but this wasn't the time or the place. She decided to try a different tactic, turn the tables on him, smother him with kindness.

"Thank you, Jordan," she offered sweetly. "I feel fine."

He grinned unrepentantly, the light of understanding dawning. Caitlin had to admit, he wasn't slow on the uptake. Never had been.

"You're worried about your looks?" He crowed with uncanny perception. "You were beautiful before. Pregnant, you're the most gorgeous woman in the place. You should know that by now."

A little bubble of mirth tickled inside her at his familiar phrasing. Caitlin shrugged. She had never been able to stay mad at Jordan for long. Perhaps he hadn't forgiven her for marrying Michael, but at least he was willing to put it behind them. For now.

"Look, Jordan, I've had a lot to deal with. And time sort of slipped away."

His stare was relentless. Caitlin knew she'd have to elaborate but opening up her heart wasn't easy.

"I'm an adult, Jordan. I am capable of running my own life. And that means *without* your interference. I'm not trying to keep your parents away. They're the baby's grandparents, they deserve to know." She swallowed the lump of fear that clogged her throat and continued, trying to explain why this was so important.

"When I tell your mother and father about this child, it will be because I want them to be happy and share it with me, so we can remember Michael together." Using her eyes, she implored him to, just this once, understand.

"I didn't want them to come racing home, cancel their plans, just to worry. I don't want them to hang around just because they think I can't handle having a baby on my own. I don't want them to think that because I was married to Michael, they have to stand in for him." She sipped her tea. "They have their own lives to lead. I'm perfectly capable of managing my life without anyone's interference."

It was a long speech and Caitlin wasn't sure even now that it made a lot of sense to him. It was hard to explain that she just knew she was supposed to do this on her own. It was her job. That's why God always took away the people she loved. So she would be strong.

"Lyn, I wasn't trying to interfere. I was just surprised." He looked up at her sheepishly. "Okay...and angry."

She stared him down.

"All right! And upset." He still sounded mad as he cleared his throat. "I had hoped..." his voice died away. "Never mind. I just thought that this one time you might accept some help," he muttered, staring at his hands.

Caitlin frowned at him. "Next time, please wait until I ask for help."

"Which you never will," he grumbled, echoing her inmost thoughts. It was proof positive that Jordan knew far too much about the way her mind worked.

"I am going to do this my way, Jordan. In my own time, depending on myself." Her eyes held his as she reiterated her plan of action in the back of her mind. "It's just the way it has to be."

"No, it isn't the way it has to be at all." His accusing stare glowed hot behind the round lenses of his wire-rimmed glasses. "It's the way you want it. It's the way you think your life has to be. Fine. Be alone. Refuse to accept anyone's help. But just remember one thing."

"And what is that?" She didn't have to ask. She knew what he'd say even before he said the words.

"Someday you're going to have to depend on someone else. And when you do—" he paused "—when that day comes, remember that you have people who are just waiting to be asked to help."

"Fine." She nodded her head. "And you understand that I want to have Michael's baby my way, the way I've planned." At his reluctant nod, Caitlin gathered her belongings. "I have to go. The next bus will be along in a minute."

She slipped her shoes on, ignoring the pinch against her toes. Taking a deep breath, she heaved herself up from the low booth.

Caitlin wasn't surprised to see him slide out or to feel Jordan's strong hand beneath her elbow, taking some of her weight as he gently assisted her. He'd always been there, making his presence felt.

"Why aren't you driving?" Concern wrinkled his forehead. "Lyn, did you have an accident?"

She grimaced. As usual, Jordan was jumping to conclusions about her. *Poor little Lyn couldn't manage.* Caitlin fidgeted, as frustrated by his consideration as she was touched. It would have been nice not to have to explain this particular weakness.

Summoning all her nerve, she met his puzzled glance.

"No, not an accident. It's just that, well, um..."
She lowered her voice and spoke the truth. "The car's
not really built for pregnant women."

He burst out laughing then, great boisterous chuckles that had the other patrons smiling benignly at
them.

"It's not that funny," she complained.

"Yes, Caitlin, it is very funny. You continue to
hang on to that decrepit heap of rusting metal regard-
less of its impracticality and all advice to the contrary.
That dinky little two-seater has been around for
ages." He shook his head, his mouth creased in a
grin.

"I've told you before what I think of a ragtop with
our frigid winters. Now you're stuck without wheels
because you can't fit into the thing." His broad shoulders shook with renewed laughter, his eyes twinkling
down at her. "Priceless!"

"I love Bertha!" She defended her car staunchly.
"And when that baby comes, we'll take rides in her
together."

"No doubt! At twenty below, with the top stuck
down, I suppose, and just to prove you can do it."

There was no point in telling Jordan that she kept
the car because it was her one and only link with the
woman who'd cared for her since her parents had
been killed in a car accident when she was ten. He'd
probably deride her for being too sentimental about a
woman who'd never shown the least bit of affection
for her.

Caitlin sighed. Maybe she was being silly. In actual

fact, the car wasn't really a gift, it was hers simply because she was next of kin. At least Aunt Lucy had admitted that much about her. And even that one familial link had been taken away.

Jordan lifted her coat from the seat and helped her into it with that special brand of care he always conferred on a woman. It was the sort of attentive thoughtfulness that made her feel special.

Caitlin supposed she should have felt flattered by his concern, but as she straightened her bulging sweater, she grimaced ruefully. She didn't feel flattered or feminine. Actually, she felt more like a Mack truck, one that was about to burst at the seams.

"How much longer?"

The low voice was just behind her shoulder. She could feel the heat of his body radiating against her as his big frame shielded her from the jostle of other customers filling the small coffee shop.

"Not long," she told him. "I can hardly wait."

"How long, exactly?" he demanded, turning her to face him.

Caitlin sighed. She'd have to tell him. She wouldn't put it past Jordan to phone the doctor himself. None of the Andrews family were exactly reticent when it came to getting exactly what they wanted.

"Six weeks from today is *supposed* to be my due date," she informed him. "But babies don't always arrive on time. I could go up to two weeks longer."

"Or you could go into labor right now." His voice was low and concerned as he searched her tired face. "You look beat."

He grinned that slow, lazy smile that spread to a warm glow and mesmerized her into agreeing to whatever he said. Caitlin blinked, trying to reassert herself.

"Come on, I'll give you a lift home. I'm not sure bus drivers know the latest in Lamaze techniques."

Caitlin smiled, softly rubbing her aching back with one hand, hoping to ease the momentary discomfort.

"Oh, right! And I suppose you do?"

Just then her abdomen hardened with a contraction. She sucked in her breath as Jordan's hands lifted her long hair free and spread it down her back.

Whew, this was a strong one. She concentrated on breathing through it, immersed in the sensation.

As he pulled her coat together in front, Jordan's hand accidentally brushed against her rock-hard midsection. Shock, mixed with sheer panic washed over his tanned face, draining it of all color.

His wide eyes stared into hers and Caitlin noted the white lines of strain creasing his face. She breathed steadily, waiting for the end of the false contraction. When it came, she drew a calming breath and moved toward the door.

Within seconds Jordan had paid the bill, rushed her out the door and propelled her over to a full-size silver-gray sedan. Moments later Caitlin was sinking back gratefully, appreciating the smooth comfortable leather interior as it curved around her tired body. Junior was settling down now, thank goodness.

She breathed a sigh of relief which turned into a startled gasp as Jordan slammed all two hundred pounds of his muscular frame into his bucket seat and tore away from the curb with a squeal of tires that would do a rowdy teenager proud.

"See an old girlfriend?" she teased, glancing at him.

He returned her look with an uptilted eyebrow that reminded her *she* was one of Jordan's old girlfriends. The one that had married his brother.

The deep groove beside his mouth kept his features frozen in a mask as his fingers clenched the leather wheel. Caitlin frowned at the obvious signs of stress. She pressed her hand on his muscled forearm.

"Jordan, what's wrong?"

"Which hospital?" he growled.

"I'm not going to the hospital," she told him in confusion. "I'm going to Wintergreen."

"Wintergreen?"

"It's the old Cardmore house. I bought it. I'm fixing it up. It's going to be a new start for the baby and me." A place where she could forget the memories and move on.

"You're going to have the baby at home?" He squeaked the words out, risking a wide-eyed glance of horror over his shoulder.

Caitlin sighed. "Pull over, Jordan."

When he kept going Caitlin cleared her throat. "Jordan. Pull over. Now!"

"What?" His strong tanned fingers still gripped the steering wheel.

"Jordan, I am not going to the hospital. I am not,

repeat *not,* in labor.'' She kept her lips from twitching only by using the utmost restraint.

''But...but...I...'' His voice died away in embarrassment.

Caitlin took compassion on his obvious distress and explained. ''That was a sort of fake contraction,'' she murmured, conscious of his gaze on her stomach. ''It happens more and more lately.''

His dark eyebrows rose in disbelief.

''Scout's honor,'' she promised. ''Doctors call them Braxton-Hicks contractions.'' She grinned at his skeptical face.

''Trust me,'' she told him in an echo of his own tone. ''I do know what I'm talking about. They've gone now.''

Jordan looked less than convinced, but when she nodded again, he seemed slightly relieved.

''It doesn't mean I'm going to give birth in your car.'' Caitlin smiled, struggling to maintain the look of solemn assurance. ''Promise.''

When his eyebrows quirked and his eyes opened wide, she couldn't hold on any longer. Her giggles finally erupted at the look of patent relief on his face.

He breathed at last, eyes closed, head bowed. Color began to return to his chiseled profile. ''Sorry,'' he said as, one by one, his fingers released their death grip on the wheel. ''Robyn pulled a 'not my time' one on me last summer.''

His high cheekbones tinged a bright pink. ''She had her baby in the back seat of my car at the hospital doors. Talk about procrastination!''

Robyn, Jordan's older sister, was famous for postponing things until the last possible moment. Apparently she'd done it once too often.

Caitlin laughed out loud at the chagrin that contorted his handsome features into a mask of dismay. It felt good to laugh again.

"It's not funny," he told her, his face mournful. "I loved that car, but I had to sell it. I could never drive it afterward without hearing her calling me names and carrying on. I felt totally helpless." He huffed, obviously affronted at the indignity he'd suffered.

"She even had the nerve to say it was my fault for not getting to her house earlier! How did I know she'd decide to get things moving just before I showed up? I only went over in the first place to visit Glen. You remember her husband?" He rolled his eyes. "I don't know how he stands her."

It wasn't easy to ignore his wounded look, but she just managed to stifle the laugh that threatened to spill out. This was something to remember, Jordan Andrews completely out of his depth.

"I promise not to do that," Caitlin told him solemnly. "Can I go home now?"

Jordan drove her home all right, at a sedate twenty miles an hour through the streets of a town in the throes of rush hour. He wasn't doing anything that would start labor he told her frankly, correctly interpreting her impatient glance at the speedometer.

"It sure is cold here," he muttered finally, cranking up the heater. "I can't seem to get warm lately."

"Yes, well, life in the tropics will do that to you. Wasn't Tahiti where you were heading after the funeral?"

"Yep, the sunny South Pacific."

"Must have been nice."

If her voice betrayed just a hint of envy at his ability to escape the mean existence of those dreadful months after Michael's death, Jordan didn't comment on it. He also never mentioned the reason he'd decided to leave so abruptly the day following the funeral. She'd never understood that, but she'd accepted it.

"So how long have you been back?"

"Actually—" he snorted in amusement "—I should be used to this weather. I've been back for a month. In the country, that is. I had a little business in New York first. I flew into Oakburn yesterday."

Caitlin pretended to study the curving riverbank. Only a few of the brilliant red and gold leaves still hung on the trees. Hikers and joggers walked through the crisp crackling carpet underfoot. And the carefully tended pathways bulged with outdoor enthusiasts taking advantage of the sunny fall weather.

Her nose caught just a hint of wood smoke in the air as up ahead a family gathered around a fire pit. A wiener roast in the park. She smiled at the memory that flickered across her mind.

"How is Robyn?" Caitlin asked.

Michael's sister had announced her pregnancy just after Caitlin had decided she was in love with Michael. Everyone in the Andrews family had been thrilled at the thought of a new baby. Caitlin knew they'd welcome Junior with open arms simply because this was Michael's child. Maybe they'd even try to take him away from her. Then she'd really have no one.

Caitlin shoved the ugly thought away with grim determination.

Jordan frowned, obviously organizing his thoughts.

"Robyn? Oh, you mean with the baby. She's fine. I still can't believe she called the kid Eudora. I called her Huey for a while. It seemed fitting—she was totally bald."

Jordan's strong fingers jerked the wheel suddenly, twisting out of the path of an oncoming motorist in the wrong lane. There was no lull in his conversation which seemed remarkable.

There wasn't a lot that fazed Jordan. Apparently births outranked everything else. She grinned again, cherishing the greenish-tinged look she'd seen on his face.

"I didn't like the other option much. Anyway, I always remember Mrs. Hatchet calling people 'dumb Doras' when they didn't catch on to her algebra lesson."

Caitlin grinned. Everyone who had been under the malevolent thumb of Agatha Hatchet had been called that at one time or another in their high school years.

"Seems too bad to saddle a kid with that kind of negative self-image label from day one." He shrugged helplessly.

Caitlin smiled. If she remembered correctly, Jordan

himself had acquired a few rather interesting tags in high school.

"There are worse things to be saddled with," she murmured. "Wasn't *Jordan the man, who rolled the van,* one of yours? And how about *Heartthrob Andrews?*"

"Well, if that isn't the pot talking to the kettle!" Those glowing eyes glittered with good humor. "I seem to remember *Cait the Great* when it came to chemistry. And *Dim Lyn* in, let's see, wasn't it history and phys ed?" A smug little smile tilted his lips.

"You tell me, Jordan Andrews...just how many of those seventeenth-century dates can you still remember?" She flushed at the old nickname, the familiar tide of indignation surging upward with the memories of those unhappy years.

He held up a hand. "Truce." He called out, grinning. "Let's just admit that neither one of us has done too badly. Especially you." He whistled at the metal name tag she'd forgotten to remove from the tip of her collar. "Doing some teaching now, huh? Do I call you *Professor* Lyn?"

Caitlin lifted her chin. She ignored the question and the reference to her newly acquired job. That had been her dream, hers and Michael's. While she'd dreamed of completing her doctoral studies as a nutrition and dietetic counselor, he had finally decided to complete his own education. More dreams that had died with him.

"You can call me whatever you want." She grinned.

There were a lot of things she preferred to forget about the old days. Her painful crush on Jordan during those high school years was only one of them. She was about to change the subject when he interrupted her thoughts.

"Well, here we are, safe at home with nary a scratch."

Caitlin glanced around, surprised at how quickly the time had gone. She hadn't even noticed they were near her home.

"I wasn't actually coming here," she muttered. "I told you I want to go to Wintergreen. I've got to get it ready."

"That old barn? Ready for what?" He frowned.

Caitlin was sure he was about to offer some unwanted advice about purchasing a huge, rambling Victorian mansion to live in, so she hurried into speech.

"I've invited some friends to live there with me. We're going to share the place. Do you remember Maryann MacGregor? She married Terrence Arnold, that lawyer from New York. Anyway, he died a while ago and she came back home to raise her daughter."

"Shy, quiet little Maryann married a hotshot, eh? Who'd have thought she'd become famous. And now she's going to live with *you*, the person who always has to be alone?"

Caitlin stuck her tongue out at him and then flushed in embarrassment. Why did she let him get to her like this? She was acting like a bratty kid.

"Not exactly live with. We each have our own

suites. Beth Ainslow and I share the first two floors and Maryann has the top floor. Beth and her sister Veronica are already living at Wintergreen."

"Sounds like fun. At least you'll have help nearby if you need it. Though, I'm not sure you should be doing much. As I recall, that place needs a lot of work. Are you sure it's safe?" Jordan fiddled with his jacket, avoiding her eyes.

"Not so much work is left now. Most of the big stuff is already done. That's partly what's been keeping me so busy. I've had walls removed and new ones put in, carpets and flooring, cabinets, the entire thing looks totally different inside."

Caitlin ignored his skeptical look. She *had* been busy. On purpose. It left less time to think.

"All we have to do is a little decorating. I'm looking forward to it."

"Well, I'm not taking you there now, Lyn. It's late and you need to put your feet up and relax." He swung open his door, his mouth set in a determined line as he strode around the car he'd illegally parked in the No Parking zone in front of her condo.

Caitlin sighed with resignation. No one could change Jordan's mind once he'd set it on something and there wasn't any point trying. Besides, she did want to get these shoes off.

He opened the door and Caitlin swung her feet out tiredly, accepting his helping hand as she stood.

"Beth's a widow, too. Her husband was killed in an accident."

Jordan didn't reply. Instead he escorted her into the

house through the sporadically swirling autumn leaves before returning with her packages.

"I think that's all you had." He set the bag down inside the door and then straightened, his eyes studying her.

"Thanks, Jordan. I appreciate the lift." She stood there, not knowing what else to say. What *did* one say to an old boyfriend who was also your brother-in-law?

"You're welcome. I've gotta go. I have to pick up some parts for my modem at the airport. I'm working on something new." Jordan bent over to brush his lips against her cheek.

"See ya, little mama," he murmured. His face peered down at her. "Take it easy. If you need anything, I mean anything," he emphasized, "just call."

She accepted his admonition and his card, and bid him good-night without promising anything. That was Jordan, she reflected with a grin, always dashing off on the trail of a new computer gizmo. It was good to know some things never changed.

She closed the door of her condo and sighed. "Pack," she ordered her tired brain. "Pack or you'll never get moved."

Hours later, after the newscast, Caitlin forced herself to bank the fire, refold her afghan and shut off the lights before awkwardly climbing the stairs to bed. Only once she was tucked up in the big four-poster with a thick comforter to shield against the north wind howling outside her window, did she allow herself to think about meeting Jordan again.

He hadn't changed much. But somehow, today Jordan had seemed more human. Less bossy than usual. Less angry. He hadn't laughed at her, not really. He'd even seemed to understand.

And he had said he would be there if she needed him.

Caitlin tugged the thick softness around her ears, allowing a smile to curve her tired mouth. It would be nice to have a friend to call on if she needed one. Even if that friend was a know-it-all, Type A personality like Jordan Andrews.

She lay there a long time, thinking about him, remembering. The rugged, jutting angles of his handsome face filled her mind's eye. A girl could get used to those strong arms and broad shoulders. Once, a long time ago, she'd even wanted to stay there and hide. But that was then and Jordan had never returned her foolish affections, not the way she wanted.

Caitlin mocked her wayward thoughts. She wasn't a little girl any more. She knew all about life. Just as you got used to having that shoulder to lean on, it would disappear and you'd have to start on your own all over again. She knew that better than anyone. It had happened too many times to count and Caitlin wasn't a slow learner.

But she was in control of her own life now, looking out for herself. It was the way the world was. She was an orphan and a widow, on her own, expecting a baby. Her husband was gone. God expected her to grow up, dig her heels in, and manage her life as best she could.

She couldn't depend on anyone else. And especially not Jordan.

She had only herself.

"It will be enough," she told herself, thrusting away the memory of those glowing gold eyes. It had to be.

Chapter Two

"I'm completely settled in at the house, Caitlin. It's great!" Beth's enthusiasm was contagious, even over the phone line. "You call me when you're ready to move anything, okay? I know lots of people who'd be happy to help an attractive pregnant little widow like you."

"Oh, brother!" Caitlin yawned, delighted to be able to relax on a Friday evening, knowing she didn't have to get up early tomorrow.

"After all," Beth added, "it'll be easier for the old poker faces uptown to keep track of us brazen hussies once we're all in the same place."

Caitlin giggled, snuggling her mug of tea against her cheek as she slouched in her favorite chair. She ignored the packing boxes scattered about her apartment.

"I know what you mean. They call us the Widows of Wintergreen. Isn't it awful?"

Beth sniffed. "At least they're leaving someone else alone when they gossip about us. That's good. Isn't it?"

Caitlin knew everyone in town expected fireworks when Garrett Winthrop finally met up with Beth, his high school fiancée. She could just imagine that the hottest topic on coffee row had reached Beth's ears days ago. She sympathized with the frustration in her friend's voice.

"They'll find someone else pretty soon, Beth. How'd your first week of business go?"

"It's been a smashing success." Beth's voice brightened. "Veronica came after school today and we unpacked those Christmas things. I can hardly wait to open officially. As soon as I get some fresh stock, that is." She giggled.

"I'm like a little kid! I've never wanted to celebrate Thanksgiving and Jesus' birth as much as I do this year. I can hardly wait. I feel as if I'm going to do really well in my first year of business."

"Good for you. Just keep that attitude, kiddo. You'll show 'em!"

Beth's flower shop was the new love of her life and she gladly shared it with anyone who listened. The fact that her sister had willingly pitched in to help get things ready was a big weight off Beth's shoulders.

"How was your day?" Beth's voice softened.

It had been twelve hours to forget, Caitlin conceded privately. Nothing had gone right. Her alarm clock declined to ring at the appointed hour, allowing little time for Caitlin's usually prolonged morning routine and no time at all to relax and contemplate her future life at Wintergreen or the advent of Jordan Andrews.

"You don't want to know, Beth. Pregnancy might increase your waist, but it does not increase your ability to tolerate certain stubborn people." She launched into an account of a client at the counseling place where she worked.

"So you didn't advise him to go back and ask Mommy for her fat-laden recipe for fried green tomatoes?" Beth giggled at the telling silence, then switched topics. "I heard you had a visitor."

The town gossips. Privacy in Oakburn was an almost impossible feat. Which was why, up until now, Caitlin had always kept mostly to herself. In Oakburn, most of the women her age had husbands and a family to keep them busy. She had friends at work certainly, but they had never become very close.

It had been relatively easy to stay a loner with Michael's parents on an extended holiday overseas, but they were back now. In fact, she'd received a call only this morning. Caitlin pushed aside the guilty reminder that she still hadn't told them about the baby. They just wanted to see her, they said. Caitlin knew it was time to tell them herself, before someone else did.

Her high school friends Maryann and Beth had come back to Oakburn within weeks of each other, and with them, Caitlin had felt as if an old connection was restored. They didn't ask a lot of questions, but she knew they were there and that they cared. It helped.

"You've been visiting the cronies on coffee row, I see, Beth. Yes, my brother-in-law Jordan is back. He drove me home last night." And stirred up a few unhappy memories while he was at it.

"Good! He can help you move your stuff tomorrow. It's time you got settled in here before the snow flies for good. That baby isn't going to wait forever."

"I know." Caitlin yawned again. "I keep meaning to do it, but something else always gets in the way."

"Procrastination is no excuse. Ask him. Right away!"

"I don't want to ask him. He'll bulldoze his way in here and take over everything. I want my move to Wintergreen to be happy, not frustrating. Jordan is just too bossy."

"Caitlin, you can do this. And from what I hear, your Jordan has a good strong back and great strong arms, which are exactly what you need."

"I don't need him, Beth," she insisted stubbornly. "I can manage."

"How?"

A long, drawn out pause hung between them.

"You find someone and find them quickly. You should have been moved and settled in weeks ago. You know Maryann and I can be over there in two minutes to help." Beth waited a moment. "Do you hear me, Caitlin Andrews?"

"Yes, mother." Caitlin hung up the phone with a smile, knowing her old friend was only trying to help.

And help wasn't a bad thing right now, she decided, glancing around the messy room.

Boxes littered the worn gray carpet. Some would go to Wintergreen, some would go to Goodwill. It was time to part with Michael's stuff, to give it to someone who could use it. It was time to move on. Embrace the future.

Why did that thought fill her with terror?

The doorbell rang. When her caller wouldn't let up on the annoying chimes, Caitlin yanked the door open, knowing from the sinking feeling in her stomach, exactly who would be standing there.

"What do you want, Jordan?" She hadn't meant to sound so cranky and immediately regretted her harsh tone.

He lounged in the doorway, a wounded look on his face. Her eyes widened at the two brown paper bags he pulled from behind his back.

"Try to do someone a favor and that's the thanks you get! I brought you dinner. Chinese food."

"I already have something on for dinner," she said even as her mouth watered at the spicy smells of egg roll and something else. Shrimp?

"Yeah, right. And I'm a monkey's uncle."

She had to smile at that. It was too good an opportunity.

"I am not carrying a monkey," she protested, knowing full well it would do little good to argue with her brother-in-law in his current mood.

"But thank you very much for the food. I'll enjoy it." Gently she eased the door closed in his startled face. His booted foot barely stopped it from clicking shut.

"Hey," he hollered. "That's not nice."

"Oh, all right. I suppose there's enough for two. Or three. Come on in," she relented, smiling as she flung the door wide.

He smiled and walked in, closing the door behind him. She knew he was ready with a smart repartee, but the words died as his mouth dropped open and he blinked while the smoke alarm began its shrill summons.

Caitlin hurried toward the kitchen. The acrid odor of burning cheese and clouds of thick smoke rendered the kitchen atmosphere blue.

'I told you I had something on," she reminded Jordan as she heaved open the window to let in some fresh air. When the noise didn't stop, she grabbed a knife and attempted to force the toaster oven to yield its charred remains of what had been her cheese sandwich. It wouldn't budge.

Jordan flicked the alarm off, waved a dish towel back and forth and then reset the unit. It immediately started its high-pitched whine again.

After dumping the smoking bits of charcoal into the garbage, Caitlin pivoted to face him. The alarm had finally stopped but left behind an aching in her temples that she didn't need. The emotions of the day rose to the fore and there was no way she could stifle her bad mood.

"I have been making myself dinner for quite some

time now," she told him. "I don't need a nurse-maid."

"Toast is not dinner," he returned calmly, stepping around her to put his bags on the table. He pulled several different cartons from the bags and set them carefully on the table. "And I know very well that Chinese is your favorite, so forget the furious rebuttal." He grinned that wide boyish smile that would make a weaker woman swoon at his feet.

"I don't listen to it anyway," he reminded her, his lopsided smirk firmly in place.

"That, my dear Jordan, is at the very root of our problems."

He ignored her frown, flopping down onto one of her kitchen chairs. "It's just dinner, Lyn. Don't make such a big deal of it."

Yeah, just dinner! Caitlin pressed a hand to her stomach, wondering how her traitorous body would react to this feast. She was starving, but had no desire to repeat lunchtime's woes. Especially not in front of him.

Morning sickness was supposed to be over months ago, wasn't it? So how come she still had it at noon when a colleague unwrapped an egg salad sandwich? Or in the evening after she'd finished a bowl of hot buttery popcorn? Why didn't anything in her life go according to plan?

She couldn't help lifting the lids, just to see what he'd brought.

"I'll just have some of the chop suey," she decided

eventually, spooning the brightly colored vegetables onto her plate. "And a bit of rice."

Surely rice would settle her stomach.

Her senses caught the vinegary-sweet fragrance of sweet-and-sour sauce as she lifted the other lids. When her tummy growled again, she gave in and ladled out three slivers of beef nestled in a glistening orange-red sauce.

"Just a little," she declared as he inspected her dish, grinning as it grew fuller by the moment. Caitlin ignored his smug look and sat down, mouth watering at the feast before her.

Jordan's murmured words of thanks to God for His goodness irritated her unreasonably. She supposed it was because she felt so tired, so abandoned. Where was God when she needed Him most? Certainly not anywhere that Caitlin had been able to find Him lately.

They ate silently together, enjoying the freshly steamed vegetables and succulent bits of pork and beef. She wasn't surprised to see there was no chicken. Jordan hated chicken in any way, shape or form.

Partway through the meal, Caitlin set up the coffeepot, giving in to a day-long craving for caffeine. More than anything she wanted a cup of coffee right now, and she wanted it to stay put in her stomach, where it was supposed to be. Perhaps then she would have enough energy to handle Jordan's bossiness.

"Do you think that's a good idea?" he asked idly from his perch on the other side of her kitchen.

All her magnanimous goodwill vanished at the peremptory remark. The stress of pretending they were good friends, that there was nothing between them, that he was just a friend, made Caitlin's blood begin to boil. It was the proverbial last straw in a day full of frustration and she whirled around.

"Yes, Jordan, I think coffee is a very good idea right now."

He opened his mouth to say something, but she cut him off before he got started on his lecture.

"Do you have any idea what it's like to be stretched so far your stomach has no room to hold your meal? To have someone constantly kicking you from the inside? To be nauseated by the very food that attracted you only moments ago?"

She clapped her hands on her hips, eyes narrowing at the amusement on his face. "Well, do you?"

Caitlin Andrews was quite a sight when she got mad, Jordan decided, admiring the sparkling green eyes and reddish flash of color in the fall of curling chestnut-brown hair. He smiled to himself, thankful to see her old spirit return.

"Of course you don't know," she raged at him. "How could you? You're a man!"

Jordan winced at the particularly nasty ring she gave to the last word. Caitlin was tired and out of sorts, that was for sure. He was glad he hadn't told his parents anything about seeing her yesterday. She was too bushed right now to handle any more than a phone call from them. He got up and walked across the kitchen, taking her arm in his and escorting her back to her chair.

She sank into it after a moment of consideration. He knew it was because she was too tired to stand. One long fingernail shook in the air at him, emphasizing her annoyance.

"Well, let me tell you, buster. I know. And I'm sick and tired of it!"

Big shiny tears welled in her turbulent green eyes. She stared at her hands, refusing to look at him. Jordan watched the tiredness swamp her body, leaving her slumped and vulnerable.

He felt like a heel for laughing at her. It couldn't be easy, having a baby. And if anyone knew all the rules to follow, it was his sister-in-law. She was a nutritionist, for Pete's sake! Jordan lambasted himself for saying anything. She hardly required him to tell her what her body needed.

He moved quickly to wrap one long arm around her shoulders.

"It's okay, Lyn. Cry it out. Soon the baby will be here and you'll be back to your old self. Everything will be..."

"Awful," she wailed, setting him back on his heels.

He shook his head in disbelief. It was amazing. Strong, capable, fiercely independent Lyn now dissolved into a soft mound of whimpers and tears. How had this happened? What was he doing wrong?

"Nothing's going the way I thought it would, Jordan. I don't know anything about having a baby, let alone raising a child." She gulped, her face pinched. "I'm scared witless at the thought of it. I grew up with Aunt Lucy after my parents died. How do I know what to say when my child asks me questions I can't answer."

Her big green eyes begged him to help. Jordan had never felt so totally useless in his life. He didn't know how to comfort her, didn't know the words to say to help her through this.

Please, God, show me what to do. Help me now, he pleaded silently.

"I'm so tired, Jordan," she continued. "Right now all I want is to be able to walk without lumbering around like an elephant. I want to do up the buttons on my clothes and not see gaps in between."

Her sad face squinted up at him. "I want to be able to sleep more than two hours at a time. Isn't that selfish?"

He patted her shoulder awkwardly, searching for something, anything, to comfort her.

"I want Michael."

Pain, sharp, sweet and condemning hit him. Jordan ignored it, as he had in the past, focusing his attention on the weeping young woman before him. He hadn't done anything wrong then. He wouldn't now. She was his brother's wife.

"Lyn, I know what you've been going through," he offered quietly, trying to calm her.

It was the wrong thing to say.

"Ooh, you are so frustrating, Jordan Andrews!" She yanked her shoulder away from his touch, eyes blazing. "You always think you know everything. Well you don't know what I'm going through at all!"

She jerked to her feet, her chair falling sideways, stopped only by his knee. He winced at the impact, brushed the heavy oak chair aside and then winced again as the chair hit the floor.

Hard and loud, the sound reverberated through the quiet room emphasizing the tension that strung out between them. He could feel the heat radiating across his knee from the old football injury. He absently rubbed his hand against the stinging flesh.

It was actually kind of funny. He'd gotten that injury because he'd been watching Caitlin instead of the offensive end headed his way. Now he'd been broadsided again.

"Oh, dear! It's your bad knee, isn't it? I'm sorry, Jordan," she groaned. "I'm really sorry." She set the chair back in place and sat down on it.

He smiled at her contrite face. "It's okay. And you're right, Lyn. I don't know how you're feeling right now. Why don't you tell me about it?"

He resumed eating. Without looking at her, he pushed the rice to one side, then spooned several more beef strips onto his plate in an attempt to avoid her eyes, waiting to see if she would open up.

"I really am sorry. I had no right to take out my bad humor on you. I should have been more careful." Her small hand reached out to cover his in a soft touch.

"It doesn't matter." Jordan sat there, feeling like

a lump of putty, mesmerized by the plucky little smile that tipped up her mouth.

"Yes, it does matter. My only excuse is that I'm not very good at managing everything yet," she explained with a tremulous smile. "But I will be. I just have to rely on myself and do the best I can." Her shoulders pressed back as she said it, as if she were drawing on a cloak of armor.

Irritation chafed him. Jordan snapped his fork against the plate with an audible *ping*.

"Lyn, there's no way you have to go through all this yourself. I'm here. Mom and Dad would love to see you. There's Robyn and the other girls. Lots of people are there, just aching for a chance to help you out. But they won't offer again. You'll have to ask."

He stopped when she shook her head.

Caitlin didn't say the words but Jordan could almost hear them in the silence of the kitchen. He knew what she was thinking, could read the words in her expressive eyes.

I've gone through that too many times. And everybody always goes away when I need them. Just like my parents, just like Michael, just like you did.

What Caitlin did say didn't make him feel any better.

"I've got to face life on my own terms and learn to handle what comes along. I can't afford to depend on other people all the time. Besides," she squared her shoulders. "I should be really good at it by now."

Jordan flinched at the misery underlying those words. He watched her push her plate away before ambling slowly to the living room. He followed silently, standing by helplessly until she sank onto the soft cushions of the sofa, her sigh piercing his heart.

"Caitlin, honey, I wish Mike was here for you. I'd give anything if he could be here to help you through this." He took a deep breath. "But since he isn't, I'd like to help. Sort of a stand-in. If you'll let me." His dark eyes met hers seriously. "Whatever you need, Lyn, you just tell me."

"I know you'd like to help." Caitlin closed her eyes, her wistful face pinched and tired. "And I know you're there, Jordan. Thanks."

But it wasn't the same thing and they both knew it.

"I know everyone thought we were foolish to marry like that, that it was too fast. I knew people thought Michael wasn't very responsible about a lot of things. That was okay, I was responsible enough for both of us." She fiddled with her hands, twisting one inside the other.

"I knew he was a terrible driver and took too many chances. But I never took any chances! Michael bubbled with life, he could hardly wait to dig in and sample everything." Her voice clouded with emotion and he watched her struggle to keep herself under control.

"But I loved him, Jordan! And I didn't care about any of that. I don't understand why he had to die. Where was God when Michael needed him?"

The tears came then, rolling down her cheeks in rivulets of emotion.

"You tell me, Jordan. Why couldn't God have left Michael to watch his baby being born, taking the first step, growing up? Why?"

Jordan sat silent, helpless, and watched her weep. Then when he could be silent no longer, he sank onto the cushion beside her and wrapped his arms around her shaking shoulders. Ignoring his own aching heart, he cradled her head against his chest.

"Caitlin, I loved him, too. He was my brother." He let his fingers stroke over her dark curls as he tried to express himself clearly. "And I don't pretend to comprehend the way the universe works. How could I, a mere human, ever grasp something so complicated?"

She peered up at him through her swollen, red-rimmed eyes and Jordan felt his heart bump in the old familiar way. Gently he pressed her back against the sofa, away from him. He searched for the words to adequately explain his faith.

"I think that life holds something wonderful for each one of us if we look for it. And that's true for you, too, if you'll only look ahead. You're doing work that interests you. You're moving into a new home. You're going to have a baby!"

He lifted her chin, coaxing her to look at him. "Yes, you've had some rough times. And there may be more to come. But you've got to believe that God loves you and cares for you enough to be there whenever you need Him. You have to trust that He will do the best for you, even if we can't understand right now."

"And you think I should *trust* someone who took away the one thing I loved most in this world?" Caitlin watched him, her eyes vicious shards of jade. "You think I should just shrug it off and move on?"

Jordan groaned inwardly as he listened to her tirade. *The one thing she loved most.* It hurt to hear her say that about Mike and not him. But it hurt more that she was still bitter and full of anger against God.

"How can I believe in something so vengeful?"

He shook his head. "No, Lyn. He is never like that. There was a reason Michael had to die. I don't know what it was. You and I will probably never know what he might have had to face if he had lived. But God knew and decided it was time for him to leave. And because He's God, He did what was best."

Caitlin shuffled a little, pulling herself up and forward. Jordan let his hand fall away.

"I know what's right, Jordan. I know all the appropriate words, all the correct phrases." She peered at him from under her lashes. "I know I should have shared the baby with your parents. Michael would have loved that."

He nodded.

"It's just that I can't seem to get there. Can you understand that? I made the choice, I put everything I had into that marriage. And He took it away. Why?"

Jordan patted her hair awkwardly, searching for the right words. "I don't know, sweetheart. But He didn't take everything. He gave you something, too, Lyn. A brand-new baby. A living memory of Michael. You owe it to Michael and his child to go on with your life. That baby is going to need its grandma and grandpa.''

''Junior's got me.'' She hugged her mounded stomach protectively.

''And he's a lucky baby to have you. But children need families. Friends. Uncles.'' He smiled, praying desperately for the right words. ''You've grieved a long time, Caitlin. It's time to live. Will you let us in now? Let us share some of the good times and the bad with you?''

She didn't say anything, just sat there, peering at him, thinking it all over. Jordan knew she would need time to adapt, change gears. He was more than willing to give it to her if it meant she would allow him back into her life.

Maybe if he went now and let her think about it, she'd realize how much she needed him. He stood. ''One of these days it's going to start snowing and it won't stop. You need to focus on the future, get ready for this baby. You're moving soon, right?''

He pulled his leather jacket from a nearby chair and tugged it over his shirt, studying her wan face seriously. ''I'll come over tomorrow and we'll get things organized.''

She smiled, her voice softly accusing. ''You always were the organizer, Jordan. That much hasn't changed.''

''Can I get the family to help?'' He held his breath, waiting for her answer. Surely she wouldn't deny them this little bit of sharing, not when she was so worn-out.

He pushed it just a tad further. "You're tired, Lyn. You need to rest. Let us help. Just this once. No strings, I promise."

She smiled but there was no bitterness in those jade depths. She seemed to have accepted that it was time to lean on someone else. Or maybe she was just too tired to argue.

"It won't be this once and you know it, Jordan Andrews." Her mouth slashed in a teasing grin. "Your mother will have everyone marching to her tune within five minutes of her arrival. The two of you are like peas in a pod in that respect."

Jordan arched one eyebrow teasingly. "And that's bad?"

"That's Andrews." She sighed, but he heard laughter hidden in the depths. "All right! I'll do it your way. Just this once."

"And can I tell them about the baby?" He wanted her to do that herself, but maybe it was asking too much.

"If you want to." She shrugged, lurching to her feet.

She pretended it didn't matter, but he knew better. Still, this one relenting bit was a step forward. And that one step was better than none at all.

"All right! What time is good? Ten?"

Caitlin nodded tiredly, one hand massaging her hip. "I suppose. I'll be awake no matter what time they come." She followed him to the door, slopping along in her floppy slippers. "I'm always awake."

"I'm sorry, honey." He stood there for a moment,

staring down at her, aching to hold her, ease her burden.

"No, I'm sorry I'm so cranky. Thanks for everything, Jordan." She offered a tremulous smile that tore at his heart.

"It's okay, Lyn. You can tell me anything, you know. It won't make any difference." He picked up her hand and held it between both of his.

Her fingers curved soft and delicate in his. Jordan glanced up, searching her tired face. A pain tightened his chest as he noted the lines around her mouth, the blue tinge under her eyes.

"Don't let the past be only sadness, Lyn. Michael loved life and he went all out for whatever he wanted. Be happy. That's what he would have wanted for you."

The rest could wait. They had time. *Please, God, give her time to accept me.*

"Remember to call if you want me. I left my number by your phone. I can be here in five minutes. Okay?"

Caitlin nodded, although Jordan wasn't sure what she was agreeing to. Perhaps she only meant she understood about the phone call. Feelings of helplessness washed through him as he closed the door softly behind him, waited for her to lock up and then got into his car and drove away in the chilly fall evening.

His heart ached to hold and comfort the young woman he'd seen peering out from those weary worn eyes. He wished he could take away some of her pain.

He wanted her to trust him. He wanted to be there for her, to share part of the burden.

He wanted to go back in time, back to a past when he should have grabbed at the childish adoration she'd so innocently offered.

Instead he'd run away, cleared the field because he'd known his younger brother was in love with Caitlin. And he'd watched while Michael had claimed her. Caitlin was Michael's wife and now she carried Michael's child.

In her current state, Caitlin wasn't ready to hear anything about Jordan's regrets. Maybe she never would be. And he could deal with that. He'd have to.

But what he wouldn't accept was that wall of distance she projected, the refusal to find the good things God had given her. Life wasn't all bad. He could show her some beautiful parts of it, parts that were bright and happy and filled with promise.

He itched to order her to relax and let someone else be at the helm for a while. He wanted to coddle her, make her feel safe. He wanted to be the one she put in charge.

Jordan mocked this ridiculous notion. He'd wager his new high-tech digital scanner that Caitlin Andrews would find it awfully difficult to let go of the controls. And he knew she'd bat his ears if she ever caught him trying to coddle her from anything. But he would be there anyway. Just in case she wanted him.

For something. For anything.

Jordan breathed a silent prayer for Caitlin as he

wove his car through the streets toward his lonely apartment. She was beautiful in a way that no other woman had ever been to him and her pain stabbed him deep in his heart.

"Help her, Lord. And help me. I can't give up on her."

Chapter Three

Caitlin opened the door the next morning to the boisterous crowd outside with a reminiscent smile. "Come on in!"

It was just like old times. Except that, back then, she and Michael had usually gone to the Andrewses'. Their sprawling split-level housed assorted numbers of Michael's family at any given time and one more was always welcome. She had often arrived for dinner uninvited and Eliza, Michael's mother, had always been just as gracious as she was now.

"Caitlin, my dear. How are you?"

Caitlin found herself enveloped by soft round arms in a loving hug that warmed her tired soul. Eliza's periwinkle eyes searched her face.

"Oh, honey, I'm so happy for you, so happy about the baby!"

Tears welled in Caitlin's eyes, her heart blooming with relief. She should have known she could trust

Michael's mother. Not a word of recrimination, no demands to know why she hadn't told them. Just friendly care and concern.

Why hadn't she told them sooner? Why was she so scared of allowing them in?

She thrilled as the trickle of warmth in Eliza's smile stimulated a ray of warmth in her frozen heart. "Thank you, Eliza. I'm sorry I didn't tell you sooner."

"There's nothing at all to be sorry for. I'm just so thankful the Lord has brought you back to us." Eliza hugged her again, her eyes tender, her arms welcoming.

There wasn't time for much else. Stan Andrews insisted on his turn at hugging *little Caity* as he'd always called her.

"I'm not so little anymore, Stan." She glanced down at her protruding stomach.

He laughed, but deep in his eyes Caitlin could see the flash of pain. It was gone as quickly as it appeared.

"All the more to love," he whispered in her ear, bringing a glow of happiness to her world. Here again, unconditional love.

She had missed them, Caitlin realized. More than she would have thought possible. But she had to be careful. No matter how friendly they were now, they would eventually leave, go on with their own lives, and she'd be left behind. After all, she wasn't Michael's wife anymore.

"Do you mind?" Jordan's distressed voice boomed

behind them. ''You're blocking the doorway, little mama.'' He had a load of empty boxes in his arms.

''If my brother starts making those gross mother-to-be jokes, just let me know.'' It was Robyn, trim and fit, elbowing her brother out of the doorway, a little blond girl on her hip.

''I'll straighten him out posthaste.'' Robyn held up a hand and waved it threateningly around his ears. ''I'm allowing no talk about weight gain today.''

''All right, already. I'm going.'' Jordan moved out of the way to put his load down in the living room.

Olivia came behind her sister, imitating Robyn's wild hand movements. Both of them converged on Caitlin, hugging her while they proclaimed their congratulations. For her part, Caitlin exclaimed over the baby as she coaxed the little girl into her arms.

While the dear, noisy, garrulous family gathered together in her tiny little living room, Caitlin let her eyes wander round. Just for a moment she allowed the joy and pleasure of it all to flow into her, rejuvenate her. She considered what she had been willing to give up and called herself a fool. This could have been hers all along.

Of course, it would be all the harder to manage alone now, having experienced the warm sense of belonging once more. But even if it was only temporary, it was worth it to have them all here again.

They were a family. Happy, loving, enjoying each other's company. And, for now, they wanted her to be a part of it. Why couldn't she just accept that and join in? Why did she feel so lost, out of place, like an interloper?

Jordan's fingers squeezed hers as the tears welled in her eyes. He alone seemed to realize how much this moment meant to her and she hadn't even heard him come close. She turned to glance at him and saw his encouraging smile.

"They just want to help," he murmured in her ear. "We just want to love you."

"Okay, children. This is the way we're going to do this."

Within minutes Eliza had everyone organized. After an inspection of her puffy ankles, Caitlin was dispatched to her bedroom to rest on the bed, feet up, while her sisters-in-law packed up her wardrobe.

"You know I've got two or three outfits left over from Eudora's premiere," Robyn offered thoughtfully. "You're welcome to them if you want a change. Although I'm certain I was ten sizes bigger than you before I delivered." She twisted and turned in front of the mirror, checking her trim figure.

"Don't worry. You've still got some left." Olivia teased her sister with a grin of commiseration as she emptied drawers. "Mom said you keep a little with each baby."

"Not me. I'm not keeping any of it," Robyn assured them both. "Next time I'm going to be extra careful about what I eat."

"I've been careful," Caitlin murmured, staring at her huge tummy. "I've done everything by the book, including exercise. At my last checkup I'd gained twenty-nine pounds. That was not the plan.''

''You're kidding! Twenty-nine?'' Robyn pulled herself out of the closet to take a second look. ''You don't look that big.''

Olivia groaned and shook her head at her sister, grinning when she noticed Caitlin watching her in the big mirror. ''Robyn always blurts out whatever she's thinking. I have to watch her.''

''I heard about some things she said to Jordan.'' Caitlin giggled, remembering her brother-in-law's face the day he'd described his niece's debut. ''He seems traumatized by your daughter's arrival.'' She burst out in delighted laughter at Robyn's exasperated snort.

''That man doesn't have the sense of a pea when it comes to having babies!'' Red spots of indignant color glowed brightly on Robyn's cheekbones. ''I feel sorry for any woman my brother marries. And woe betide her if they ever decide to have children. She'll probably knock him out before it's over. And he'll deserve it!''

Caitlin glanced at Olivia, who rolled her eyes and shrugged.

''What happened?'' Caitlin finally asked, smothering her giggles with great difficulty.

''He told me to stop being such a wimp! Can you believe it? As if that great lummox could even imagine pushing a nine-pound watermelon out of his body! The man has no compassion.''

''None at all,'' Olivia agreed, smirking at Caitlin

behind her sister's back. She leaned down to whisper. "He told her that having a baby was a perfectly normal, natural thing for a woman to do."

"Well, I suppose it is," Caitlin murmured, frowning. She wouldn't have said it, but she couldn't argue with his logic.

"Maybe. But no one in their right mind tells a woman doing hard labor that women in some countries have their babies and then go immediately back to the field and finish their work. Not if you value your life."

"And not if that woman is Robyn," Caitlin agreed, remembering that Michael's sister was particularly sensitive to pain. "We'll have to give him the benefit of the doubt then. Jordan wasn't in his right mind."

Olivia burst out laughing, then clapped a hand over her mouth. Caitlin knew exactly what she meant. She could picture the two of them, brother and sister nattering at each other as a baby waited to be born. It was something she could only dream about.

"She called him names," Olivia said, loudly enough for her sister to hear. Her eyes still sparkled in merriment.

"And he deserved every one of them." Robyn was stout in her own defense, her voice emerging muffled from inside the closet. "Control myself indeed! As if I had any *control* over Eudora's arrival!"

Caitlin couldn't help it. She let the laughter break free. Just then Jordan's curious face peeked around the door and she giggled all the harder, tears rolling down her face as he frowned at them.

"Is everything all right?" he asked Caitlin, ignoring the other two women. "You're not in pain or anything?"

"You mean pain, as in labor?" Robyn's snarl was only half pretend. "And what would you do if she was?"

When Jordan's face blanched, Caitlin burst into renewed gales of laughter, joined seconds later by Olivia. It was evident he didn't relish the prospect.

"I'll get Mom." He gulped.

"Don't bother. Caitlin is fine. *I* at least, know how to treat pregnant women," Robyn informed him smartly. She smacked a group of hangers together and laid them in a box. "Go and do some wonderful hulking-man thing like tossing around furniture, Jordan. You're not needed here."

"What did I do to you?" He scratched his head, peering at his sister through lenses that were smudged and dirty. "You think you'd appreciate me a little more since I assisted your daughter into the world."

"You what?" Robyn pushed her way free of the clothes, hands on her hips as she glared at her brother. "I dare you to say that again."

Olivia rushed to the rescue, tugging her brother's arm to get him to move out the door. "Uh, this isn't a good time to bring that up, Jordy. Come back later. Or better yet, wait till we call you. Don't call us. Okay?" When he frowned at her, Olivia stood on tiptoe and pressed a kiss against his cheek. "I love you, big brother, but you're not doing yourself any good here. Go away!"

The order was just audible enough that Caitlin heard every word. She saw Jordan shake his head, obviously confused.

"Okay, if you think so."

"We think so!" Robyn added her two cents' worth.

Jordan frowned and then retreated, his golden eyes puzzled at her sour tone. "I'll see you later, Caitlin. Alone." He glanced from her to the other two, then left, muttering to himself.

"He's impossible once he gets an idea in his head." Robyn rolled her eyes, her tone confidential. "As if he helped! I don't know where he gets this stubbornness from. None of the rest of the family is like that."

Those words were so far from the truth, Caitlin burst into renewed chuckles, her heart warming to these wonderful women. How had she stayed away so long?

More important, what would she do when the novelty wore off and they left her on her own?

Olivia and Robyn arranged her jewelry, clothes, lingerie, socks and shoes in several boxes and then urged her to move from the bed.

"We've got to get this bedding off before they come for the mattress. Dad rented a trailer and he and Jordy are going to load everything onto it and haul it over when Glen comes this afternoon. Then we'll get you settled in. Wintergreen, Jordan said?"

Olivia's eyes glowed, begging for information. "I heard there are going to be three of you. It sounds like such fun. Can I come once in a while for some girl talk?"

Caitlin nodded slowly. "Sure, Olivia. Anytime. But

I'm hoping it won't be just us girls for long." She saw Robyn's head jerk back at the same time that Olivia flopped on the bed beside her.

"Why? What's going on?"

"I'm going to try my hand at matchmaking," Caitlin told them smugly. "But you can't say a word to anyone. If the old gossips on coffee row get hold of this plan, they'll spoil everything."

Eliza wandered in, a list in her hand which she consulted after a glance around the room. Olivia beckoned her over.

"Listen to this, Mom. Caitlin's got a plan to match up her roommates with husbands. You're good at that, you can help."

"Of course I can help," Eliza agreed smugly. "I got Robyn married off, didn't I?" She preened a little in front of the mirror. "That was my biggest coup so far."

"Hey!" Robyn half frowned, half laughed. "I didn't need your help to marry Glen."

"Of course you did. You just didn't *know* I was helping you. If it wasn't for me, the two of you would still be arguing over who has the better job, reads the most books, and things like that." She ignored Robyn's gasp of outrage.

"Now, what's your idea, Caitlin?" Eliza's eyes opened wide, innocently.

Caitlin quickly explained about Beth's husband, the man she'd married on the rebound. "Then he was killed and Beth and Veronica had to move out of the company house. Beth was left with a mound of debts, it's a miracle she can still smile. It's a terribly sad story. And Beth's had such an awful life anyway."

"What do you mean?" The women were all ears.

"She doesn't talk about it and the only thing I know is from when we were in school together. I got the impression that Beth and her sister didn't have the happiest home life. She was always afraid to go home when we were out with youth group, and if she was late she'd get all shaky."

Caitlin stopped, remembering her own youth with an aunt who had never cared when she came or went as long as it didn't cost money and there wasn't any noise. She and Beth made good soul mates, she decided grimly.

"The poor dear. Of course, I barely remember the family. I was so busy with the children in those days. Five children were enough to keep anyone busy." Eliza shook her head. "We'll be happy to help you however we can, Caitlin. Certainly Beth needs to find someone who can love her the way God meant."

"Oh, b-but, I didn't mean for you all to get involved," Caitlin stuttered, aghast at the thought of these managing-Andrews meddling in the delicate affairs of the heart.

"Of course we want to be involved! I can't stand to see anyone unhappy. Now what about the other girl? Mary something, isn't it?"

"Maryann." Caitlin gulped. What had she unleashed with her careless tongue? "Maryann Mac-Gregor. But she's not, I mean, I don't want, that is, she's already in love with someone."

Oh, no! Now she'd blurted out Maryann's most private secret. And she didn't know it for certain. Not really. It was just that a funny soft look came over the woman's face whenever she saw Clayton Matthews. That plus the fact that they'd been really close ten years ago made Caitlin suspect an ember still burned. All she wanted to do was fan it a little.

"Well, that's just wonderful, dear! How kind of you to help things along." Eliza held out one hand and helped Caitlin off the bed. She pulled a chair forward and pressed her into that while still speaking.

"But first things first. We can't possibly help out with someone's love life until we get *you* settled in your new home. You just sit there and relax, dear. Olivia, I want you to start on the kitchen. Robyn, you finish packing the books in the living room. Then we'll have lunch."

Caitlin sat where she was told, stunned and filled with disbelief.

What had she gotten herself into? She'd meant to get her friends together in the nicest possibly way. A hint, a few words to the right man. Maybe a chance encounter that wasn't so chance. Just a few little things to encourage her widowed friends to reconsider a couple of men she happened to know were interested.

But this! This would turn into an all-out assault campaign, not unlike guerilla warfare. In spite of her protestations, she knew it was snowballing out of control even now. That was the way Eliza did things. Stan claimed that her brain concocted schemes even though her body was sleeping like a log.

It was true! At this very moment Caitlin could feel Eliza's mind whirling as she turned from the doorway, her eyes intensely scrutinizing Caitlin's burgeoning body.

"Hmm," the older woman murmured, her pen tapping against the pad. "Widows. Right. Three of you. I'll have to think about that."

Fear and trepidation filled Caitlin's mind. She would probably ruin the only friendships she had left. Then she'd be well and truly alone in a house that was far too big for one woman and one tiny baby. While everyone bustled out with a box, she sat there brooding.

"Caitlin?" Jordan flicked on the overhead light. "What are you doing just sitting here? Is something wrong?"

"Everything," she whispered, clenching her fist at her side. "Absolutely everything."

"What do you mean?" His face blanched. "What's wrong? Is it the baby?" He waited, shifting impatiently from one foot to the other as he waited for her to answer. "Caitlin?"

She glanced up dazedly, an idea forming in the back of her mind. "It's your fault, Jordan," she whispered. "You're the one who insisted I have them over here. You're the one who said I needed their help."

"And?" He frowned. "What's wrong with that? Honestly, sometimes you make no sense, Lyn. The moving is going really well."

"That's nice," she murmured, nodding absently. "It's a good idea to get it down to a science."

"It is?"

"Yes, it is. Because unless you help me get out of this mess, I'll be moving back here in a matter of days."

He slid his hand along her forehead, checking the temperature. "Caitlin, are you feeling all right? Can I help?"

"Oh, yes," she asserted, lurching unsteadily to her feet, her fingers tightening around his helping hand. "You offered and I'm taking you up on that. You're going to help, Jordan. You're going to end up helping me a lot."

"Help you do what?"

He didn't pull away, but Caitlin could feel him flex his fingers in her tight grasp. She didn't loosen her grip in the slightest.

"I've opened a Pandora's box, Jordan. And now you've got to help me get the lid back on before your family ruins everything. What you're going to do is keep your mother away from Wintergreen. If that means you have to come over every day, so be it." Caitlin tumbled it around in her mind as the plan evolved. "She won't bother me nearly as much if she thinks you're filling in for her."

"Huh?" He stood where he was, shaking his head. "I don't get it."

"Oh, you will," she assured him, a tiny smile lifting the edges of her lips. "You most certainly will."

Chapter Four

"**Y**ou're late, Lyn," Jordan chided Friday night, almost a week later. He straightened from his leaning position against his car and took her arm to walk her to the front door of her new home.

"I know. Two clients showed up after their scheduled times." She opened the door and ushered him into the foyer. "I just want to change and then we can leave. Where are we having dinner?" she called over her shoulder.

It took only a moment to unlock the door and then they were inside. In the days since Jordan had reentered her life, eating together had become a ritual. He would either show up on her doorstep with take-out food or insist on escorting her to a restaurant. He claimed it was because of his mother. He'd even shown up once for lunch, drawing surprised stares from her co-workers. Now her friends Beth and Maryann were full of questions.

"Have a seat. I'll be down in a few minutes." She scooted up the stairs to change clothes.

In some ways Caitlin was grateful for Jordan's attentions. She hated cooking after a long day at work and would have happily settled for hot buttered toast and tea even though she knew the folly of such a diet. Under Jordan's insistence she ate a nutritious dinner without all the work of preparing it and none of the tedium of cleaning up afterward.

Then too, there was Eliza. As long as Jordan kept coming over, his mother seemed perfectly happy working on the Thanksgiving decorations for the annual fellowship supper. Caitlin felt confident that if she could only keep abreast of Eliza's doings, as reported by Jordan, and keep herself out of her mother-in-law's path, she couldn't possibly divulge any more secrets. The fact that Eliza sent Jordan over to Wintergreen on the most minor of things didn't bother Caitlin at all. In fact, it was nice to have him to talk to.

But some evenings, like tonight, Caitlin would have preferred to stay at home and read a book in front of the roaring fire in Wintergreen. The old house seemed to wrap its arms around her and she'd felt comfortable there from the first night.

"Lyn? Hey, did you hear anything I just said?"

Jordan's voice from the bottom of the steps pulled her from her musings and Caitlin tugged on her maternity pants, sweater and sneakers without further hesitation.

"Be there in a minute."

"How about Giorgio's?" he called up the stairs.

"Sounds fine to me." She took a deep breath and let the busyness of work drain away. "I'm ready."

An hour later, she stared at him across the table in a low-lit family restaurant. It was comfortable but not intimidating and she loved the wonderful pasta dishes Giorgio's served.

"What did you do today?" she asked, curious about his work. Since he had bounded back into her life, his days seemed to be full of plans for bigger and better computer systems.

"Let's see. We got that contract in London for the security order, so I've been trying to map out exactly how soon we can fill those needs."

A tremor of fear coursed through her veins. "Does that mean you're going overseas again?" she queried softly, half afraid to hear his answer.

"Nope." He grinned that boyish smirk that made him look younger than his twenty-nine years. "Bank securities are my partner Devon's specialty. When the times comes, he'll go."

Caitlin relaxed and then realized that what she really felt was relief. It wasn't a good sign. She couldn't allow herself to rely on Jordan. Or anyone else. God intended for her to manage things herself.

"I've got a deal pending in Banff that could be a biggie if I can land it," he told her as they discussed the computer firm Jordan and his friend had built up from scratch.

Caitlin listened as he described a satellite system that would monitor vast areas of the mountainous terrain enabling park rangers to uncover potential forest fires and tourists lost in remote terrain, in record time.

After several minutes, she was lost in the intricacies of engineering such complex equipment. She sat, dreamy eyed, content to let him ramble on, basking in the warm pungent aromas of garlic, tangy tomato sauce, baking cheese and yeasty bread sticks.

It was several seconds before she realized Jordan had stopped speaking. Instead he was peering at her with a look of concern on his face.

"Are you okay?" His voice was soft. "Having more of those hiccup things?"

Caitlin smiled. "No, I'm fine. And they're Braxton-Hicks contractions, not hiccups."

She waved a hand at the groups of families scattered through the busy restaurant, their happy chatter a hum of noise in the bustling restaurant.

"I was just thinking of a girl I've been counseling. She would give almost anything to be here, with her father, having dinner." Caitlin fingered the water glass on her place mat. "Actually, Addie reminds me a little of myself at her age," she admitted.

Jordan grinned. "Oh? She's stubborn, too?"

"No. It's because she's an oddball. Like me."

His gold-flecked eyes studied her seriously. "Caitlin, you are not an oddball."

"Yes, I am. Or at least I was. I never fit into the high school cliques. Now I just plain don't fit into anything." She giggled at the silly joke, pushing a length of her hair behind her ear as she eyed her bulging tummy, but Jordan didn't laugh.

Her brow furrowed in concentration as she chewed on her bottom lip, striving to clarify her meaning. "I was different, you see. And nobody had to tell me that. It was something I knew. I didn't have a family like the other kids, I was just staying with my aunt because there wasn't anybody else who wanted me. After school, when the others dumped their homework and went out for a shake, I toddled off to my job."

"Lots of kids have jobs, Caitlin." Jordan countered.

"Yes, they do," she agreed. "And many enjoy them. That's not what I mean."

He shrugged. "I don't get it."

"Not every kid feels they have to contribute something or they'll lose their home, Jordan." Caitlin shrugged avoiding his eyes. "I felt I had to earn that money so Aunt Lucy would keep me, so I wouldn't be a burden. In some sort of weird logic I figured if I made my own money, bought my clothes, looked after things, she wouldn't mind having me there so much."

She watched the furrow on his forehead deepen as he considered her words.

"I'm sure your aunt was happy to have you there, Lyn. She was a lot older, I know. But I don't believe she ever meant to make you feel beholden or unwelcome. You probably imagined that. She just wasn't used to having a child around."

Caitlin nodded thoughtfully. "Could be," she admitted. "Things get skewed when you're a kid. I withdrew because I didn't like my own reality. I didn't think much about her side of it, I guess.'' She munched on her bread stick for a few minutes, trying to discern reality from her memories.

"Addie's like that, too. When we discuss her food choices from the week before, it's simple to see she's camouflaging her feelings by overeating.''

"I suppose everyone does that.''

"Maybe. For a time. But when it goes on long-term, it's denial. That gets serious.'' Caitlin threaded her fingers together and then, when she realized what she was doing, laid them in her lap.

"I recognize it because I did the same with my aunt. Lucy wanted a calm, quiet retirement, and I tried to give her that. I didn't feel comfortable inviting anyone over, and I sure wasn't in with the group who held sleep-overs. I used my books to escape.'' She smiled softly, remembering those fantasy stories.

Jordan stared perplexedly at her. "Used your books?''

Caitlin realized he wasn't following her meaning. How could he? Jordan had a big, loving family. He was far too involved with his life to need the illusions fairy stories would provide. Besides, Jordan always dealt in the here and now, in reality.

"When people, teenagers especially, don't have a real sense of security, they often move into a fantasy life. Mine was in books. And food.'' There was no way to describe those deep, secret longing for happiness, she decided.

"But Lyn,'' he protested. "You were smarter than

anyone else in school. You were years ahead in most subjects.''

''Yes. But that wasn't as great as it seemed. When you add to my insecurities the fact that I was two grades ahead of my peers, had nothing in common with my classmates and that I was overweight to boot, well—'' she grimaced ''—it wasn't a solution for successfully handling what life throws at you. I ended up hiding the real me and falling miles behind my peers in developing my own personality.''

''How did you figure all this out?''

''I talked to a counselor back in my undergrad days. She helped me see that I was compensating for losing my parents. Her words, not mine.''

Jordan shook his head. ''I can't believe I didn't see anything,'' he muttered. ''I was in the same school. I even worked on the same newspaper.''

Caitlin grinned. ''And all you saw was *the brain*, right?'' It was reassuring to see the glint of teasing in his dark eyes. She brushed his arm with her hand.

''Don't worry about it, Jordan. You were a teenager, not my adviser. You had your own problems.'' She wished she hadn't let it all out, let him see how insecure she'd been. It was time to lighten up. She peered up through her lashes. ''I can't seem to remember you suffering from anything other than girl problems!''

His face grew darker then and she laughed at his chagrin.

''Ten years later and you're still embarrassed about being the school heartthrob?''

"Listen. I had problems like everyone else. But I sought my counsel in the Bible."

"Oh, please. I do *not* want to hear about that!"

Jordan removed his glasses, wiping the lenses with his napkin as he glared at her, golden eyes filled with warning. "Fine. But I think," he said firmly, "that's enough talk about me. Let's hear how things are going at the house. Did you get the baby's room finished?"

"Nag, nag, nag. No, I did not. I've been busy."

"Doing what?"

"I'm helping out a friend." She avoided his eyes.

"Not Clayton Matthews?" He frowned when she nodded. "Again? What is it that the two of you are doing, anyway?"

"Oh, I'm just showing him a few things."

Caitlin had no desire to explain how totally clueless the farmer was when it came to matters of the heart. Not that she had any great knowledge! But anyone could learn to dance and socialize and Clayton did seem desperate to gain the attention of Maryann. He just hadn't had much success in relaxing in her company.

"*Showing* him?" Jordan's eyes darkened. "What do *you* need to show a man like him?"

"He's very shy. I'm just trying to help him get over that so he can ask someone out." Caitlin glanced around the room, hoping he'd drop the subject.

"Maybe I should talk to Clayton. Give him another man's perspective."

"No!" Caitlin immediately lowered her voice,

fully aware of the interested stares from the other patrons. "Clay would never forgive me if he thought I'd told anyone about this!"

Jordan put his fork down and studied her face intently. His forehead furrowed in a frown. "I don't like any of this, Lyn. You insisted I help you, and I've tried to keep my family out of the way. But my mother's been asking a lot of questions and it's getting harder to put her off. She keeps wanting to know if you're going out with anyone, if you're having dinner alone, if you need some odd job done. That kind of thing."

"You have to put her off. If she finds out about Clayton and me she'll get involved and that would ruin everything." The very thought of Eliza jumping in to match up two reticent people like Clayton and Maryann made her cringe.

"Mom might be able to help."

Caitlin shook her head firmly. "Uh-uh. No offense, Jordan, but your mother couldn't keep a secret if her lips were taped shut and her hands were tied behind her back." She smiled to show she wasn't serious, not completely anyway. "It's important to me."

"Important to you?" Jordan's glowering face was full of questions. "Just what is this man to you, Caitlin?" The chill in his voice set her hackles raising.

"Oh, for Pete's sake! Not you, too." She whooshed out a breath of disgust and straightened. "I've already got half the town plotting to match the Widows of Wintergreen up with some unsuspecting male. If they guess why Clayton..." She shook her head, her imagination taking over.

"I'm not trying to match anyone up," Jordan growled. "But you spend hours with the man. Good grief, what are we supposed to think?"

"You're supposed to think that I'm trying to help him get up enough nerve to ask out the woman he's loved for years! That woman is Maryann MacGregor, not me. And you're supposed to believe it because that's what I told you." Caitlin tamped down her indignation.

Small towns, she thought with disgust. Everybody was always trying to make something out of nothing. It was so frustrating. If they kept this up, Maryann would soon notice Clayton's comings and goings! Caitlin suspected her friend wouldn't appreciate her efforts, no matter how kindly they were meant.

Maryann had been in the limelight too long. She'd returned to Oakburn with the intention of leaving the cameras behind. Caitlin shuddered to think how upset the shy, reserved woman would be if she knew people had been talking about her.

"I suppose the next thing will be finding someone for Beth Ainslow?" Jordan pushed his plate away, his eyebrows drawn together.

Caitlin took a sip of water, unsure whether to tell him her thoughts or not. He didn't seem very sympathetic. And besides, what did he care if she was busy the rest of her life?

"I don't know if there's a lot I can do for Beth. She's very kind, very bouncy, very..." she searched for the right word "...up. But she's hiding behind that. It's not easy to get her to talk about personal things."

"Sounds like normal reserve to me."

She ignored that. "Besides, Garrett Winthrop is still nursing a grudge. It's not going to be easy to get him to forgive and forget."

Jordan's gaze settled on her, something glinting in their depths. When he finally spoke his voice seemed faraway. "Sometimes it's just not that easy to forget the past." One hand reached out to brush a lock of hair away from his eye. "Sometimes the past looks a whole lot better than the future."

Caitlin frowned, wondering what he was talking about. Did he mean Garrett and Beth, or was he talking about the two of them and the fact that when she'd needed him, he'd sent Michael to her.

"Jordan, I..." She didn't know how to tell him what was in her heart, didn't know whether he regretted his actions or not. Maybe it was best to leave things be.

"Sorry." His voice was low and apologetic. "Let's change the subject. What are you planning for tomorrow? You don't have weekend clients, do you?"

"No." She shook her head and then waited while their server set down the steaming platters of lasagna. "Oh, this is great. I'm starving!"

He grinned. "So what's new? What about this girl you mentioned earlier?"

"Addie. She's making progress but it's slow. She

doesn't feel very secure in herself and that causes a lot of problems.''

"I thought you said her father was some wealthy businessman? She doesn't have to worry about money or security." He frowned. "What does bother her?"

"It's complicated, Jordan." She shrugged, neglecting to mention that Addie's problems made her reflect on her own. "I'm still studying her, but basically she just doesn't feel loved and she's trying to get her father to prove he does."

"Ah." He nodded with understanding then sprinkled Parmesan cheese liberally over his pasta. "Her father's away a lot, I suppose?"

"A whole lot. He tends to use his secretary as Addie's mother and she, of course, feels abandoned so she tries to prove that she's worth loving." Ouch, this was getting too close to home. Caitlin clamped her lips closed and concentrated on her food.

Jordan was silent for a long time, picking at his lasagna absently as he considered her words. When he finally looked up there was a softness about the chiseled features.

"You know, I grew up in a home where my parents treated us as people, a part of the circle of their love in spite of our faults. Somehow I never felt I had to measure up to anyone. I always felt they just wanted me to be the best me I could be. They seemed happy with that."

His eyes stared ahead unseeingly. "I realize now just how much of a gift that acceptance was when I hear you talk about this Addie.'' His glance shifted to Caitlin.

She could almost hear him say ''and you.''

''But I can't help feelings that Addie needs someone to rely on. Someone who will be there for her when she runs out of her own power. I think she needs to find someone to put her trust in. Someone who won't let her down. I think she needs God.''

''I don't think religion is going to solve all of Addie's problems, Jordan.'' Caitlin heard the skeptical tones in her own voice and mentally winced. There was no point in offending him just because *she* had a problem with God.

''No, not a religion. A relationship with God. And I'm not saying all her problems will disappear. But when you look at it, none of us are really great human beings. We need someone to depend on. Everybody has some little flaw they try to hide from other people.''

Caitlin grinned. Opportunities like these weren't to be passed up. ''Even you?''

''Yes, even me, I suppose. Though I don't have many and most of them have already been corrected.''

She chuckled, enjoying the repartee she'd missed for so long. ''Your sisters think there's work to be done.''

He sniffed. ''They should take care of their own colossal imperfections before looking at my few faults.'' He slid a hand onto the table, his face growing serious. ''Everyone needs to know that there is someone there, to trust in and to believe that they'll come through."

"That's what I just said. You've learned to deal with life." Caitlin savored the rich tomato flavor, happy that she'd given in to his persuasion and come along. This was very relaxing.

"No, Caitlin, it's more than just 'dealing with life.'" Jordan hunched over the table, his fingers entwining together as he tried to make her see his point.

"I don't have to worry about pleasing someone else all the time, trying to fit his or her mold, because I've already learned that I am important to God. That's the first big hurdle to acceptance."

He ignored her arched eyebrow. "The difference is that this Addie sounds like she's trying to get through everything on her own. She can't do it. Or if she can, it will only last for a while. People need God and other Christians in their lives to help validate them and the choices they make."

"And what about when those Christians fail?" Caitlin wasn't talking about Addie's father now. This issue was a little too close to home. She had a feeling Jordan knew it, too.

"Everyone fails now and then. It's called being human. You get up and move on."

Caitlin bristled, realizing he was directing some of his comments at her. It was so easy for him. He didn't have to worry about being alone, depending on himself, making mistakes. There was always a crowd of people hovering around in the Andrewses' household.

"Not everyone has dependable people in their

lives, Jordan. And sometimes the people you do depend on leave you high and dry.''

Jordan nodded. "Quite often, in fact. That's the beauty of having faith. Things will work out. You just have to be patient and trust that God has something special for you. You have to *trust* Him.''

Caitlin paused before she said anything. She didn't want to hurt his feelings, but neither could she just let this pass. "Jordan, I don't think I believe that anymore. Michael's gone. It's not going to get better.'' She sipped her ice water in an effort to control the frustration that whirled within.

"God let me down with Michael, just like He did with my parents all those years ago. They died, my aunt died, and Michael died. God could have stopped it, but He didn't. And no amount of faith is going to bring them back. Now I've got to learn to stand on my own two feet.''

Jordan was silent for a few minutes, obviously deep in thought. She reared in surprise when his next words came.

"Caitlin, would you believe God hadn't let you down if Michael had survived the crash and was lying in the hospital in a coma?''

"It's hypothetical,'' she murmured. "But at least there might be some hope.''

"Even if the doctors said he would never regain consciousness?''

Caitlin shuddered. "No, I wouldn't want him to just lie there, with no possibility of ever waking up.''

Jordan nodded. "Would you feel better if Michael had lived but been paralyzed, then?"

She hated this. "I don't know."

"What if he was in constant agony, but still alive?"

"I've said I don't know," she replied tersely, laying her fork on the table. "Why do you keep asking me these awful questions?"

"Because we can't second-guess life, Lyn. And, no matter how much we want it, we will never know why Michael died. No explanations, just reality."

"It's awfully hard to accept that." She bit her lip.

"Yes, it is hard," he agreed. "But we can get through it. With God's help. And friends." He cleared his throat. "I miss my brother every day. But I know that where he is has to be a far better place. I have to let God take care of him and get on with my life. Someday I'll see him again in heaven."

His smile lit up his eyes as he spoke and Caitlin found herself mesmerized by the lilt in his voice.

"You see, Lyn, the difference is where we put our faith. You want to put yours in yourself. You think if you do enough, be enough, work hard enough, you'll be okay. But if something knocks you down, your house of cards tumbles and it takes a long time to rebuild."

"And?" She avoided his eyes.

"I put my faith in God. He's all powerful, all knowing, all seeing. We make a strong team. What I can't handle, He does. And He gives me faith in myself and my friends." His hand covered hers. "When

I get bowled over by life, He's still there, waiting to help me up.''

Caitlin reconsidered Jordan's words as they finished dinner and then during the short silent car ride home. She continued to think about things long after he'd brushed her cheek with a friendly kiss and left her inside her door.

Was she really strong enough to be everything to her child when she herself felt so needy?

The answer was simple. She had to be.

But how?

Caitlin brushed the problem away, unwilling to probe that question too deeply. Grabbing a nearby pad of paper, she began to list the essentials that had to be completed before the baby arrived. This, at least, she could get a grip on, she told herself. *This* was under her control.

Chapter Five

Saturday morning dawned bright and clear. It would be the last really good day of autumn, Caitlin decided, eyeing the baby's nursery with dismay,.

Where had the time gone? She had intended to have Wintergreen, her apartment, and especially the baby's room, ready at least a month ago. With a little more than a month before her due date, it was high past time to get the painting done. And the weather had provided the perfect opportunity to do so. The unseasonably sunny, clear day meant she could open the windows and allow the nontoxic paint fumes to escape while she worked.

But before she could even begin, she was interrupted by a knock on the front door.

Jordan asked her as he stepped inside, "What are you going to do this fine day, Mrs. Andrews?"

"I'm painting the baby's room." She ignored his

gasp and stepped around his big frame to walk toward the nursery.

"Caitlin, you can't paint a room in your condition," he admonished her loudly, following behind.

"I can paint if I want to! I have to get it done before the baby arrives." There he was, bossing her around again.

"Yes, but breathing paint fumes isn't—"

"Mr. Becker at the hardware store said the paint I chose doesn't have that problem." She glared at him furiously. "I'm not totally helpless, Jordan. Good grief, even I can paint a room."

"Can I help?"

"Jordan, I'm not helpless. I can do this." She stopped when his head started shaking.

"Yeah, I know that," he told her, staring down at his shoes. "It's just that, well, uh..." he cleared his husky voice.

Caitlin stared, unsure of this new side of him. She had never seen Jordan so at a loss for words before.

"I just thought, maybe I could be, well, part of the preparations? You know? Help get things ready for my new little niece or nephew."

His eyes had melted to a deep bronze. They were soft and molten like liquid gold. She saw tenderness but no pity.

"Kind of, well, step in for Mike."

The softly spoken pledge tugged at her heart. Jordan wasn't bullying or ordering now. He just wanted to be a part of things. Against her better judgment, she gave in.

"Okay," she agreed finally. "But no telling me how to do things. I have something in mind and you're not changing it, Jordan. Not one little bit!"

He acceded easily enough, the twinkle of mischief back in his eyes. And to his credit he said nothing when she teetered on the rungs of the ladder, reaching for the crease along the stippled ceiling. He merely stood below, his lips pursed in a tight, straight line, holding the ladder. Nor did he comment when she dripped paint into his hair. Or when she wavered with dizziness on the second from the top rung.

But when she finally came down off the ladder, he was there with a cold glass of water.

"Sit down and drink this," he ordered.

As she watched, his face assumed that tight mask of control, devoid of any visible emotion. She hated that look.

"I'll take my turn now." He took the roller from her without asking and climbed the ladder, his lips pinched together.

Caitlin drank the cool refreshing water thankfully. And when it became clear that Jordan had no intention of relinquishing his hold on the roller or the ladder, she took the brush to the corners, filling the seamed areas his roller didn't cover.

They worked in silence as the fresh autumn breeze blew in the windows. It helped carry away some of the nontoxic paint smell and Caitlin was grateful.

But eventually she had to get out of the room. Her aching head and queasy stomach refused to subside and since Jordan had insisted the bedroom door remain closed to seal off the rest of the house, it was impossible to get totally away from the odor as long as she remained in the room.

"I think I'll go make some tea." She left with an admonition for him to call her when he needed help. Once downstairs, Caitlin headed for the front door to check the mailbox.

"Hi. What's up?" Maryann stood in the front hall, the area that divided their apartments. "Got company?"

"Jordan." Caitlin made a face. "I'm trying to paint the nursery and he insists I leave it to him. That man is so bossy." She grinned. "But to tell you the truth, I don't know what I'd do without him. At the moment I've got a splitting headache."

"There's nothing wrong with having someone care about you, Caitlin," Maryann murmured.

"Yes, I know. It's just that Jordan sort of bulldozes me into things. And I don't even realize it until he's left." She frowned. "I've got an idea for that room and I intend to carry it out."

The doorbell rang then, cutting into their conversation.

"That's for me," Maryann said. "Amy and I are going out."

"Oh." Caitlin's interest perked at the mention of Maryann's daughter. "Going with anyone I know?"

"Everybody seems to know everything around here," Maryann chuckled as she tugged open the front door. "Come on in, Peter. I'll just get Amy. Peter's Amy's skating coach for ringette."

"Okay. Hello, Mrs. Andrews." Peter Bloomfield stepped into the hall, his smile white and gleaming.

Caitlin nodded absently, wished him a good day and then turned back into her apartment. She closed the door carefully, her mind busy. Seconds later she had the phone next to her ear.

"Clayton? Maryann and Amy are going out with Peter Bloomfield. I thought we agreed that you would ask her out. Dancing, you said."

The bachelor's quiet tones rumbled down the phone line. "Oh. Yeah. Well, I tried. But I just couldn't do it, Caitlin. Maybe after a few more practice sessions."

All that time she'd spent encouraging him and he *still* wasn't sure? "All right, Clayton. If you're certain?"

"Yes. Yes, I am. Can I come over for lessons again?"

"Yes, all right. Monday night. Bye, Clayton." Caitlin hung up the phone with another sigh.

"He's coming over *again?*" Jordan stood frowning at the bottom of the stairs. "What's it for this time?"

"He's not quite confident yet. He feels he needs a few more sessions before he makes a move."

"What kind of sessions?" Jordan's face was dark. "Are you counseling this guy or something, Lyn?"

"No. If you must know, I'm trying to teach him to dance." She held up a hand. "Please, Jordan, I can't say any more. He made me promise, so don't ask. Just make sure your mother doesn't happen to drop over for coffee on Monday evening, okay?"

Jordan didn't say yes. But then he didn't say no, either. He just stood there, glaring at her, before he turned and went back up the stairs.

"Did you want something?" she called.

"Yes," she heard him mutter, his voice grumpy. "But I don't think I'm going to get it." Seconds later the nursery door slammed shut.

Caitlin shrugged and walked out into her tiny kitchen. She watered the herbs that had started to sprout in the windowsill planter and realized her headache was easing.

Some time out of that room was all she needed she told herself, ignoring the muscles that protested from the effort of too much unaccustomed reaching.

Time out and some time away from Jordan Andrews was the best possible solution to her problems. Lately he had a way of looking at her that made her strangely nervous. A quiver would start in her tummy and zap to her brain, rendering her mental functions virtually useless.

It was a schoolgirl reaction and she ordered herself to get over it. Jordan was handsome and kind and sweet. He'd help out anyone in her predicament. And, after all, she *was* his sister-in-law.

At twelve she went to call him for the small lunch she had prepared. She found Jordan whistling as he rolled on the last few strokes.

"You're finished, already?" she said, amazed at the difference a paint job could make. The walls glowed smooth and creamy in their new coats of velvet gloss.

"It's not that big an area and the surface is in good shape."

"It should be. I paid a small fortune for a plasterer."

He avoided her eyes as he covered an area she'd already painted earlier. His smooth even strokes blended out the lines left by her hurried determination to do it herself.

"This is where I'm going to put the duck decals," she told him happily, holding up her hands to frame the area.

It was amazing how quickly the feature wall evolved after that. Jordan suggested a light-blue background for the space behind Mrs. Puddleduck.

They walked downstairs, still discussing the nursery.

"She needs a pond," he told her seriously, his eyes gleaming through the paint-spattered metal rims of his glasses as he stood in the kitchen. He washed out the roller while she served the soup.

A pond sounded reasonable.

"Okay," she acquiesced. "But that's all. No more frills. I want to do ruffly curtains and with the border I bought today, that should be enough accents. The furniture I ordered will complete it."

They ate without speaking, enjoying the relative calm of their lunchtime, munching on the cold cuts and rolls she served.

They sat for a while and then Caitlin moved to the sofa where she could feel herself drifting to sleep.

When she awoke, she realized Jordan had covered her with the teal afghan from the living room.

The dishes lay stacked neatly in the kitchen sink. And there was a faint sound of whistling from upstairs. She followed that sound and found Jordan in the nursery, surrounded by small colored cans of paint. She also saw that the mural had expanded from a simple pond to include three white, puffy clouds floating in a pale blue sky.

"Atmosphere," he told her. His eyes were fixed on the wall, studying it as if something were about to emerge.

Shaking her head, Caitlin went to get him some coffee. When she returned, an array of bright-yellow daffodils waved on thin green stalks from a clump of warm-brown dirt on the edge of the lake.

She hadn't finished admiring those when he added two thick green trees and a patch of high reedy grass. She called a halt then.

"Jordan, you can't put on any more. There won't be room for Jemima Puddleduck or her brood!"

His eyes were glazed as he stood back, studying his efforts, paintbrush in hand. "A boat," he murmured. "A little sailboat with a bright-red sail, maybe."

"No, no more. It looks wonderful just as it is."

He didn't appear to hear her. "I think if I..."

Caitlin took the brush from his hand and tossed it into the garbage bag. "If you've got so much energy, you can help me put up the border along the ceiling edge," she muttered. He agreed readily enough and once he'd finished his coffee, they began pasting the bands of color onto the newly painted walls.

"Are you sure we shouldn't wait before doing this?" she asked him for the sixth time. Her hand swept over the wall, assessing its condition. "This paint does seem dry enough."

"It was dry ages ago," he reassured her. "Otherwise I wouldn't have started that." One long finger pointed to the scene he'd created.

"Here's another one. We're almost done," she cried exultantly as he placed the last bit carefully against the wall.

They picked up the bits of paper and glue that clung here and there to the pale-gray carpet. Finally Jordan went to wash while she called the baby store to request a rush delivery of the furniture. It suddenly seemed urgent to get the room finished.

To her surprise, the store manager said they could bring everything within the hour. Caitlin could hardly control her anticipation as she surveyed the room, mentally placing the items she had chosen earlier in the week.

When she couldn't wait any longer and Jordan had returned, she insisted that the walls were dry enough. They lifted up the sticky characters and applied them, using great care to avoid smudging the freshly painted mural. Jordan continued to speculate.

"Perhaps a beach ball," he deliberated. "And a pail and shovel."

"No, Jordan."

"But Lyn, if it's a boy, he'll want some boy toys."

Caitlin was losing her patience. "Jordan, we're talking about a newborn baby here. Toys will come a little later, okay?"

He nodded absently, his mind obviously somewhere else. "I really think a boat…"

"Jordan," Caitlin muttered, tugging the change table Robyn had given her through the door to its place under the wall lamp. "Jordan?"

He was on his hands and knees staring at the bottom of the grass. "You know—" his dark eyes beamed up at her "—if we just put a little garter snake here…"

"No," she bellowed, repulsed by the very idea of a snake in her baby's room. "No reptiles!"

His merry chuckles made her flush with embarrassment.

"I was only teasing," he muttered, unabashed when she fired off a glare.

They worked together with the delivery man, her directing and the men lifting as they moved the oak crib and an antique rocking chair Caitlin had purchased to just the right place and then moved them again because the ambience wasn't quite right.

The chair she finally placed near the window so she could see outside. A tall bureau found its home strategically situated near the change table to allow her handy diaper swaps.

At last everything was where she wanted it. Caitlin gazed round the room with satisfaction. It was a beautiful room. And it had taken half the time she had expected to ready the nursery. Thanks to Jordan. She turned to meet his dark gaze.

"Thank you." She felt as if her whole body was smiling with the relief of having this job done. "I appreciate the time you've spent here, helping me." She smiled softly. "You've made this room very special. I value your help."

He grinned back, bowing at the waist. "My pleasure, Caitlin. I enjoyed every minute."

His face grew more serious as he studied her through his spattered lenses. "I think you're going to enjoy sitting in here. And the baby will love it."

A wistful look covered his face. Then, like a cloud, darkness flooded his eyes. "I just wish you would consider allowing the rest of the family to help a little more. Mom and Dad would love to be on call for whatever you need."

The goodwill and harmony they had just shared evaporated now like the sun behind those dark wintry clouds that had started blowing in from the north. Caitlin turned to leave, tugging the black garbage bag behind her. When Jordan took it from her, she let him, not saying a word. Her footsteps were weary as she plodded slowly down the stairs. He followed silently.

But Jordan wouldn't leave it alone. She knew him well enough to know that he was like a dog with a bone once he got hold of an idea. And right now, the last thing she needed was more tension. Life already seemed like she was walking a tightrope. Quarreling with Jordan would only make it worse.

"I promise, I'll involve them in the baby's life.

They'll be so tired of me, they'll beg off. But not right now, okay?''

"But Lyn, they'd love to..." He took a second look at her face and stopped talking.

As she sank into the big armchair, Caitlin's brain searched for a way out of her dilemma. She did not want to have this discussion again. How could she tactfully explain that she was afraid their interest wouldn't last, that she'd become a burden on them, that they reminded her of what she'd lost?

Nothing momentous occurred to her by the time he broke the silence.

"Why don't you come over to Mom and Dad's for supper tonight? The girls are planning Dad's birthday on Sunday. They'd love to see you again.''

Caitlin recognized the veiled reference to the fact that she had studiously avoided his family. Jordan, it seemed, was intent on making up for lost time. Two visits in one week?

"I know they're a bit talkative and my mother does have a slight tendency to stride in where angels fear to tread." Jordan winked. "But if it gets to be too much, I promise I'll take you straight home. Inquisition or not.''

"Okay," she agreed softly after several moments of rapid thought, eventually admitting the real reason for agreeing to his plans. She wanted to see them again, revel in the love and caring. "But only if you phone your mother first and tell her I'm coming.''

"Fine," Jordan grunted, obviously satisfied if not mystified by her sudden capitulation. "I'll phone her, but you know perfectly well that she loves company. The more the merrier.''

"And tell her we'll bring over some chicken, too.'' Jordan groaned his dismay, his face curled up in disgust.

A scant hour later they were waiting at a local fast-food establishment to pick up the fried chicken Caitlin insisted on ordering. Jordan climbed out of his car with reluctance, only to poke his head back in at her.

"I hate chicken, you know,'' he muttered, his wide mouth curving down in distaste.

"I do know, Jordan.'' Caitlin grinned at him without apology. "And even if I didn't, you've reminded me at least six times since we left home.''

"Why couldn't we just pick up some steaks and barbecue?''

"Because I feel like eating fried chicken. I'm sure your dad will have something else, just in case. He doesn't seem to enjoy this particular delicacy any more than you do.''

"That's what I'm afraid of,'' he groaned. "Dad likes some really wild things. What if it's bear sausage?''

She grinned. "Maybe it will be roasted pelican or unruffled duck. Will you stop wasting time and just get the chicken?''

"Fine. I'll go, but I don't like it.'' He shoved his hands in his pockets, his hair flopping down over one quirked eyebrow. "How come you don't eat pickles and ice cream like the books say?''

"You read books about pregnancy?" The very idea sent her eyes winging to his.

"I'm interested. Okay?" Jordan flushed a deep, dark, embarrassed red. He sauntered into the store, mumbling to himself all the way.

Caitlin sat in his car and considered this newfound knowledge. Jordan was reading up on pregnancy. It was...endearing. Imagine taking the time to study her condition! The knowing warmed her inside until she considered the folly of what she was doing.

She was letting them in. Little by little Jordan and his family were eating away at the protective wall she'd built around her heart.

"But it's only temporary," she assured her nagging conscience. "Just till after I get settled with the baby. Surely it's not wrong to be friends with Jordan. Is it?"

But is it friendship you want from him? Or are you looking for a replacement for Michael? Is Jordan just a way of avoiding the truth?

"I know I'm alone here, God," she muttered, dashing the tears from her eyes. "You don't have to hit me over the head. I know that there's only me I can count on."

I'm here.

The words resounded through her head like a train whistle in a tunnel.

You can depend on me, Caitlin.

"No, I can't," she whispered, twisting her hands miserably.

I will never leave you. I'm always here.

Could she believe that?

Chapter Six

A half hour later, ensconced in his mother's front room, Jordan allowed his eyes to rest on Caitlin once more. Her hair curled down her back in a riot of dark russet that refused to be confined. Her clear profile was both elegant and arresting. She was as beautiful as she had ever been.

Caitlin's eyes, dark and mossy, almost hid the fears and secrets she never talked about. He'd been acquainted with her for years and yet Jordan realized he had never really known her at all. When she was hurt or worried, Caitlin pulled inside herself. That was exactly what had happened when Mike died. She had closed herself off to everyone.

Those same eyes seemed duller now. The dimples remained though, hidden away at the corner of her mouth until she grinned that impishly heartrending smile that stretched her wide full mouth and tore at his heart.

Jordan turned away, calling himself a prize fool. Caitlin was his brother's widow. She was lost and alone because his brother had died while driving Jordan's car.

Rationally, in some part of his brain, Jordan knew it wasn't his fault. Michael had always driven fast. And the terribly cold conditions last winter made black ice a sure thing. But nothing he told himself, and nothing anyone else could ever say, took away that niggling bit of doubt at the back of his mind.

Should he have died in his brother's place?

He was brought out of his introspection by the slap of his father's hand on his shoulder.

"Come on, son. We've got to get those buffalo steaks seasoned and on the grill if we're going to eat tonight." He chuckled at Jordan's quick look toward the kitchen. "I, for one, refuse to eat chicken."

The hint was subtle, and Jordan surged to his feet as Stan had known he would. "Chicken, yuck. Those are the magic words, Dad," he whispered conspiratorially. They sneaked out while the women chatted and admired the newest antics of Robyn's daughter Eudora.

As they sat out on the deck, watching the northern lights wave and flicker in the black autumn sky, Stan questioned his son's sudden silence. "What happened to the life of the party?"

"I don't know," Jordan replied, then teasingly turned the question around. "Are you tired or something?" He grinned at his father's smug look. "Maybe your age is catching up with you. Or maybe it's the peculiar food you eat. Has Mom been feeding you Scottish haggis again?" He ducked to avoid the swat Stan directed at his head.

They shared sympathetic male glances of commiseration.

"She looks good, doesn't she Jordy?" They both knew who Stan was talking about.

"Yeah. Better than she did this afternoon, anyway." Jordan filled his father in on the now ready nursery.

"Why'd she keep away for so long, do you think?" Stan asked, his lined brow creased in thought. "Michael's death should have drawn us closer."

"I know, Dad. But Lyn's always been a loner. Remember that her folks died when she was little and she was left with that old aunt of hers for company. I guess all that kind of built up over the years and she feels isolated." Jordan followed the white ribbon of light as it folded and rolled across the dark sky, turning green, then fading away.

"When Lucy died, she left everything to her next of kin, that is, Caitlin. Never even named her. Not a very loving gesture to the girl who lived with her for so long. I suspect Caitlin doesn't really understand the bond between families."

Stan nodded, his voice soft with affection. "At least she's got the baby, son. That'll help her."

Jordan shook his head. "I'm not so sure the baby's a good thing for Caitlin right now, Dad. I'm not even sure she's really over losing Michael."

When Stan's white head reared back in surprise,

Jordan tried to explain himself. "It's not that I'm not happy about Michael's child being born. I think it's great." He stared into the night trying to organize his thoughts. "It's just that Lyn's going to bank everything on this child, you know. He or she is all Lyn has left and her emotions are all wound up in that responsibility, in proving herself."

He took in a lungful of the cool, fresh air and tried to explain more clearly. When the harvest moon slid out from behind a cloud, Jordan could see leaves floating down to earth.

"Lyn is going to have to be both mother and father to this child and the idea scares her. I think that's why she's backed away from you and Mom. She's afraid she won't measure up or something. She hasn't had a role model for a long time, remember?"

His father studied him wordlessly, his look thoughtful.

"Since her parents' death, Caitlin never had anyone who made her feel extra special. Then Mike came along to look after her, be her protector. Now she's lost him and gained the responsibility of a new life. I'm not sure that what she needs are more worries. I think what she really needs is a childhood." Jordan grimaced at his father. "Twenty-six is awfully young to take on all those burdens alone."

"It's awfully young to die, too, Jordy," Stan murmured softly, reminding him of Michael's youth so quickly gone. "But we can't question God. If He's going to be in control, we have to let go and trust Him to work everything together for good."

"I know, Dad, I know." It wasn't anything Jordan hadn't been telling himself for months now. "I don't understand, but I'll try to trust."

Stan straightened from his position with a groan, kneading the small of his back. "You know, son, if Caity never had a real loving home, then she's never had the security of love that comes from a family like you and Mike had. She probably never found someone who cared about her until you guys came along. You two must have been like some kind of knights to her back then."

Jordan broke in with his own thoughts, his face heating with embarrassment. "I wasn't that, Dad. She just had a crush on me. It was Mike she really loved. In fact, other than that short time she shared with him, I think she's spent most of her life on the outside, looking in."

"So you've said before. But, Jordan, the thing is..." Stan stopped and stared up at the stars that glittered above. "Maybe the purpose of us in all of this is to make sure Caitlin finds out what it's like to have love backing her all the way. Maybe if she feels she can rely on the rest of us, she'll be able to let Michael go."

Stan met his son's clear gaze head-on. "I think Caitlin is going to need us now more than ever. She's a strong young woman, but nobody can do it all. Only God can do that." His father grinned slyly. "Maybe you'll be the one Caitlin will lean on again. That should please you."

Jordan thought about his father's advice as they

pulled the buffalo steaks off the grill and took them inside. He thought about it as the family ate dinner. He considered every aspect of having Caitlin lean on him, allowing much of the conversation to ebb and flow around him.

A faint smile curved his mouth as he considered the likelihood of feisty, determined Caitlin Andrews leaning on his shoulder. It wasn't apt to happen anytime soon, but he couldn't think of anything he would like better.

Caitlin perched on the corner of the huge double bed Stan and Eliza shared, admiring the quilt they'd come up to see. She'd been aware of what was coming when Robyn offered to load the dishwasher so they could "talk." Now Eliza's hand folded around hers.

"Honey," the older woman's soft voice comforted. "I'm not complaining, but I wish you had told us sooner. So we could have helped you. It must be difficult for you."

"I'm sorry," Caitlin apologized, feeling silly for doubting their warm reception and yet still needing to hold on to her reserve. "I should have. I just wanted to make sure I could do this on my own, I guess." She met Eliza's probing blue eyes. "I feel I have to stand alone, be strong. Besides, you were busy."

"Not that busy! And you are strong, dear. The strongest young woman I've ever met. But sometimes it's okay to lean on other people, too. At least we're here now and you won't be able to push us away. We're going to keep you really close.''

There wasn't a hint of censure in Eliza's smooth voice as she hugged her daughter-in-law, just a wealth of warm, unconditional love. She held no grudges.

''Now tell me,'' the older woman commanded, smiling. ''Did you have a lot of morning sickness?''

''No, thank goodness. I was never really sick, just sort of woozy some mornings. The oddest thing still sets me off.'' Caitlin rolled her eyes back in her head. ''Of course, some foods have the power to make my insides flip,'' she acknowledged with a grin.

Eliza nodded. ''I know exactly what you mean. I craved onion rings with Robyn, but one taste and that was it.''

Caitlin giggled. ''I just get the slightest whiff and whoosh…there goes my stomach. Hamburgers do it every time.''

They laughed together at the vagaries of pregnancy and Eliza still held her hand as they wandered back downstairs.

''I love having you here,'' she whispered, a tear in the corner of her eye. ''It's like having my other daughter home after a long absence.'' She tucked a strand of hair behind Caitlin's ear and smiled. ''Shall we see what Jordan's up to?''

As they walked through her home, Eliza related a few stories about her five attempts at motherhood, including Jordan's unexpected arrival.

''He was early, you know. Almost a month.'' Eliza winked as they returned to the kitchen to find the two men playing chess and sipping coffee at the kitchen table. "But then, Jordan's always been pushy," his mother teased. "Never could wait his turn."

"I've noticed," Caitlin replied tongue in cheek as she watched her brother-in-law sprawl across the table, reaching for his king. With a wing of dark hair dropped over one eye, Jordan resembled a mischievous little boy. He stared up at them through his lenses, one hand dangling over the chessboard.

"Were you two talking about me all this time?" he speculated, puffing his chest out. "Of course, there is a lot to say."

He assumed a wounded look when they burst out laughing, but bore their teasing with reluctant good grace. He offered a few choice witticisms of his own that had them clutching their sides just as Natasha, the youngest of the Andrewses' daughters, stuck her head through the kitchen door, closely followed by Olivia.

"Caitlin," Natasha squealed, enveloping her in a hug before standing back to survey her sister-in-law. "You look great. Big, but great."

Robyn groaned. "I've just cured Jordan of foot-in-mouth disease, Nat, and now you start. Olivia, feed her a cookie, so she'll stop embarrassing us."

Everyone began chatting at once and Caitlin sank into a nearby chair, enjoying it all.

A few moments later Eliza questioned her daughter. "What have you been up to tonight? You look like the cat that swallowed the canary."

Natasha grinned her big toothy smile and shrugged

her elegant shoulders, dislodging her white wool cape. She hung it on a nearby peg then smoothed a hand over her suede pants. As buyer for a women's boutique in nearby Minneapolis, Nat always wore perfectly coordinated outfits in the latest styles. Caitlin envied her chic look.

"Oh, just trying to get the rest of my Christmas shopping done," she said, plugging her ears when the entire room began to protest.

"Good grief," Stan grumped, using his son's favorite expression. "It's barely the end of October. What's the rush?"

"Oh, you know Nat. Always be prepared. Good thing she's going out with a Boy Scout." Jordan put in his two cents' worth with a smug look. He clutched his chest in pretended pain when his sister glared at him, her eyes daring him to continue.

"Ow, that look hurt!" He burst out laughing when she ignored him. "You're such a bully, Nat."

"Just because you never get around to doing any shopping until four o'clock on the twenty-fourth," she reminded him with a sniff, "is no reason to make fun of everyone else, brother dear. Some of us are organized." Her wide eyes beseeched Caitlin's in mock despair.

Caitlin couldn't suppress a grin. They were like little kids.

"You know, Caitlin, the man is almost thirty years old. You'd think he would have figured out by now that Christmas comes on the same day every year."

"What day is that, Nat?" Jordan kept his tone perfectly serious as he moved his knight one step closer to Stan's king.

"See what I mean," she wailed to Caitlin, eyes sparkling.

I see, Caitlin thought to herself. I see that you love Jordan as much as he loves you.

That thought started a little ache in her heart. There was so much love here, she could feel it surrounding her, nestling her inside its warmth and protection.

"Checkmate!" Jordan snapped his piece onto the board, then crowed with delight, rubbing his hands together with glee while his father sat frowning and confused.

Stan protested, glowering as he studied the board. His eyes searched for some devious means that would explain his son's sudden success.

"You cheated Jordan. I don't know how, but you did. There's no way you could have pulled that off!"

"Cheated?" Jordan's big grin drooped. He thumped a fist to his chest. "You wound me to the quick!"

"If you mean your heart, it's on the other side," Robyn chastised, but her lips twitched. "And you did take advantage of Dad. We just don't know how. I think you should get closed-circuit TV, Stan."

"As if you know anything about chess," Jordan sniffed disparagingly.

"Children," Eliza pleaded, although her face was wreathed in smiles. "No fighting when company is here."

"Caitlin's not company," Jordan denied. His big grin warmed her chilled heart. "Caitlin is family."

"That she is, son," Stan agreed. He pushed the board away, then stood to press a light kiss against his daughter-in-law's cheek. "That she is. As my daughter she should learn how to play chess, don't you think, Eliza?"

Eliza nodded absently. "I suppose so. Though it's a rather boring game, I always think."

When Stan and Jordan would have protested at such heresy, she cut across their objections by urging everyone into the family room. Minutes later she and Robyn passed around her special blueberry pie and ice cream. As they ate, they talked, one voice over another, changing subjects faster than lightning. At one point Caitlin found herself involved in three separate conversations. She couldn't help but grin when Stan got so involved in Olivia's story to her that he ignored Jordan's diatribe completely.

"Yes, but you don't understand politics," he chided his daughter, a twinkle at the back of his eyes. "Women always take it too seriously."

"It is only our country, after all," Caitlin teased, watching Olivia's eyes. "No point in getting all hot and bothered about a little thing like that." She burst out laughing at Stan's guffaw of disgust.

"Where's Glen when I need him anyway?" Stan grumbled, searching the room for his son-in-law.

"He's working late so he can take the weekend off," Robyn informed him. "And you two don't agree on politics anyway."

"We'd agree about this," Stan blustered.

As the controversy raged, the entire family got into the act. There was no acrimony, no hard feelings, no overruling of one by the other. They bickered and squabbled good-naturedly while the last of the pie magically disappeared off Jordan's plate.

"I saw that," Caitlin whispered.

He nodded. "I know. And you're not going to tell a single soul. Particularly not my dad. Right?"

"Or?" For the first time in a long while Caitlin felt really alive, a part of something. She narrowed her gaze. "What will you do?"

He thought about it for a few moments, his forehead pleated in a frown.

"Well?"

"I don't know yet." He licked his fork clean, then slipped his empty plate behind him on the bottom shelf of the nearby coffee table. "But it's going to be really, really bad."

"Oh, no! Now I'm *really* scared," she giggled, feeling the years roll away as she teased him.

"Good." His fingers laced through hers and he leaned back on the sofa, pulling her against the cushiony softness, his shoulder touching hers. "I suppose I'll have to keep you here beside me, just to make sure you don't blab."

"I suppose." She relaxed, content to be quiet and observe the give-and-take of love that flowed so easily in this family.

"Hey, Caitlin, are you awake?" Robyn turned the focus on her.

Jordan shook his head, watching Caitlin smother a yawn. In seconds he was on his feet, reaching out a hand to pull her upright. "Right now Caitlin's too tired to listen to you silly girls any longer."

The female contingent rose en masse in protest.

He blithely ignored them all, tugging Caitlin toward the front door. Once there he dug in the closet, found what he wanted, then placed Caitlin's thick coat over her shoulders.

"Time to get the little mommy home," he whispered for her ears alone.

She frowned at him, knowing it would be absolutely no good whatsoever to rant at him for his bossiness. Who said she wanted to leave? What she wouldn't give for a little more height and a really authoritative tone right now. Unfortunately she was just too tired to argue. Instead she accepted his outstretched hand that held her gloves, tugged them on and walked obediently to the door.

"I always said he was pushy," Robyn muttered to her mother as they gathered around.

"It was a lovely evening," Caitlin murmured, hugging her mother-in-law goodbye. "I'm glad I came."

"I'm glad, too," Eliza whispered back. "I just wish I had some free time to discuss that girl with you. Mary something, isn't it?" She frowned. "We need to get cracking on some plans for her and that shy young man. It's just that I've been so busy lately. Jordan's looking after you, isn't he?"

There was an odd look on Eliza's face that Caitlin didn't understand. But there wasn't a lot of time to think about it and she brushed the nagging questions aside. Eliza was involved in her own life. Wasn't that what she'd wanted?

"I've tried to make sure he gets over there every day to check up on you. It gives him something to do and then we know you're okay. Otherwise he'd come over here and eat all my pie." Eliza's bland smile made Caitlin giggle.

"He thinks no one noticed," she whispered.

"Of course he does. But mothers always notice." Robyn hugged her too.

"If you need me, you just call, Caitlin. I'd come over more often myself, but I just can't spare the time right now. Besides, you've got Jordan." Eliza said it triumphantly, as if the very idea thrilled her. "Since he's home, he can lend a hand. I know he doesn't mind and there's so much to do in the church. It'll soon be Thanksgiving!"

"Don't forget, Mom, I'm doing the pumpkin pies for our dinner," Robyn announced, her eyes glinting with mischief.

"That's nice, dear. Don't forget to put the spices in this year, will you?" Eliza glanced over her shoulder to be sure her daughter heard, then turned back to Caitlin.

"Of course, Caitlin, if you need something moved or rearranged, Jordan can help with that, too. He has plenty of muscles and they need a good workout now and then. He does far too much sitting around, staring at those computers of his. It's not healthy."

"I do work out!" Jordan frowned, affronted by this

slur against his physique. "And I'm very healthy. Aren't I, Dad?"

Stan shrugged. "I don't think it's healthy to eat so much pie that you try to hide the dishes," he quipped as he leaned down to kiss Caitlin's cheek. "Bye, dear. Don't feed Jordan, okay? He's getting a pot belly."

"I am not." But he couldn't resist checking his midsection in the hall mirror in spite of the smothered laughter. "You guys, I am perfectly healthy!"

"If you say so, dear." Eliza ignored his grumpy tones. Instead she focused on Caitlin, wrapping a scarf around her throat. She buttoned the top button firmly and then stood back to admire her work.

"There, now. At the first sign of labor, you call *me*, Caitlin. Jordan will be no help at all. He's not good at handling pain." She winked a big blue eye at the officious hand her son had wrapped beneath Caitlin's elbow. She didn't lower her voice at all. "But don't tell him I said that."

"No." Caitlin agreed with a smug little smile. "It wouldn't be fair to let Jordan know he's not great at everything." She smiled at his snort of disgust.

The girls all wished her goodbye. As Natasha hugged her, she whispered, "We didn't overwhelm you, did we?"

So that's why she and Olivia had come later than the others. They'd been worried about her. Caitlin felt a nice steady glow of love inside.

They left the house with good wishes and demands for a return engagement ringing in their ears.

"I hope they didn't wear you out," Jordan's deep

voice broke into her musings as they walked to the car.

Caitlin rubbed her abdomen absently, wondering why the baby always chose late at night to exercise. Jordan held open the door and she climbed inside, glad to relax against the seat. "Of course not. I like your family, Jordan. I've missed Robyn and Natasha and Olivia."

His dark eyes studied her solemnly, his voice softly mocking. "They've been there all along, Lyn. All you had to do was phone."

There was no condemnation. He simply closed her door, walked around and climbed inside as if nothing untoward had happened. The engine started on the first try and soon they were moving, slipping into traffic without difficulty.

"I know it." She threaded her fingers together. "It's my own fault I've been alone. I guess I thought I deserved it." As she said the words, Caitlin realized how lonely she had been for the friendly banter and warm friendship that was so much a part of the Andrews family.

They both fell silent as Jordan negotiated the car through the busy streets. It wasn't an uncomfortable silence, though. More of a companionable pause in the conversation. A short time later they were pulling into the driveway of her home.

Once inside, she slipped her feet into a pair of soft terry slippers, enjoying the snug feel of the soft fabric against her cold toes. Tomorrow she'd buy a new pair of warm, sturdy winter boots, she decided, hanging up her coat and closing the closet door as a waft of fresh cedar filled the hall.

"I'll light a fire, shall I?" Jordan stood inside her living room, patiently waiting for her answer.

"Yes, please." She smiled as he walked over to the big stone fireplace and removed the wrought iron screen. "I like having a fire."

Caitlin glanced around the room, admiring the hominess. There was something about coming back to Wintergreen that cheered her up, warmed her soul. Was it because she knew the others were here, that she wouldn't be alone? Or was it, she wondered guiltily, because she'd run away from the place where Michael had lived, laughed and loved? Was she trying to escape her past?

Sinking gratefully into the comforting depths of the sofa, Caitlin lifted her legs onto a nearby hassock. She sighed with relief.

"Problem?" Jordan turned from his kneeling position in front of her fireplace. The flames licked at the paper and kindling he'd laid.

"Just calisthenics time." She smiled. "This kid always chooses the evening to start bouncing around. I hope it's not a precursor of things to come."

She glanced back at him shyly only to find Jordan's dark gaze fixed on the tiny movements outlined on her abdomen by the thin fabric of her top. As he stared, Caitlin thought she detected a flicker of something in his eyes. Longing?

"Do you want to feel him?" she asked without

thinking, totally unprepared for his immediate response.

"Yes," he agreed rapidly, sliding the grate into place before striding over to where she sat. He squatted down beside her, his face telegraphing his discomfiture, letting her know he wasn't quite sure of the next move.

Caitlin grasped his big hand in hers and placed it over the rise of her tummy while her eyes remained glued to his face. The baby chose that precise moment to deliver a walloping belt.

Jordan sucked in his breath, his eyes swiveling to hers. Caitlin couldn't help but grin at the wonder on his face.

"That's just a warm-up," she told him solemnly.

"Does it hurt?" His dark head tilted to one side as he stared at her through the clear lenses of his wire-rimmed glasses.

"Uh-uh," she denied, sucking in a breath as her abdomen contracted into a hard lump. She closed her eyes to concentrate on the feeling, breathing in and out rhythmically. "Just kind of like a cramp."

Jordan's hand moved in a gentle circle. His voice was so soft, so gentle and full of love, Caitlin barely heard the words as he spoke to his niece or nephew. The voice was mesmerizing and hypnotic, brimming with compassion. She closed her eyes and let it wash over her.

"Whoa, there, tiger. Your mama has had a long day. Take it easy now and get some sleep." His hand kept up the gentle, soothing stroke until the contraction had vanished. The baby gave one more vigorous poke before settling down.

"That's the way. Sleepy time. Good baby." His deep voice died away.

Caitlin opened her eyes to find his face peering into hers, his lips mere inches away. A look of stunned wonder held his dark eyes wide.

"It's a tiny little miracle," he whispered. "Too fantastic to understand. Thank you for sharing it with me." His lips grazed her cheek for just a second before he moved away, surging to his feet with leashed energy.

Caitlin sat frozen, afraid to move. Afraid that if she did, she would fling her arms around Jordan's wide shoulders and bawl her heart out.

It hurt, it hurt so much. To know that if he'd offered just then, she'd have let Jordan into her life, no questions asked. What was wrong with her? How could she betray Michael and his memory like this? How could she even think of Jordan as this baby's father? Was she so weak, she'd lean on anyone, rather than get through this herself?

The questions bit at her like condemning ice pellets, demanding that she face the broil of emotions inside. Caitlin refused to listen any longer. She needed a diversion. When Jordan offered to make tea, she agreed. As he walked toward the kitchen, she got up to listen to the answering machine and hopefully regain some control.

"Caitlin, it's Garrett Winthrop. I'd like to speak to

you. In private, if you can manage it. Call me, please?''

''Caitlin, it's Beth. He called again and he's really upset. Oh, Cait, what am I going to do?''

One more beep.

''Mrs. Andrews? This is Ferd's Music. Uh, it's about those songs you asked for, the ones your aunt had. The only way we can get those songs anymore is on some old, secondhand records. Not too many people want CDs of that stuff and, like I told you before, we're not up on that old time music.'' A pause. ''So do you think you want old records or what? Should I keep on looking?''

By the sound of his voice, Ferd Weatherby thought he was dealing with a woman two bricks short of a load. And maybe he was. What made her think Clay Matthews would do any better dancing to old music?

Caitlin met Jordan's careful scrutiny when he returned with her brown Betty teapot. He poured out two cups, set one down on the coffee table and motioned her to sit. The other he carried with him to his chair.

''Who left you those messages?''

''My, er, projects. They, um, want my help.''

''Projects? As in more than one?'' he queried, one eyebrow tilted upward ''I thought it was just Matthews.''

''It is. Or it was. Now Garrett Winthrop wants to see me, and Beth needs to talk. They used to be an item once.''

She took a sip of the tea he'd poured, grimaced, then quickly returned the cup to its saucer.

"Is something wrong? I thought you liked sweet tea?"

Though she searched his eyes, there wasn't a hint of malice there. That meant this disgusting concoction had to be an accident.

"Yes, I, er, I do." She left the cup where it was, barely able to swallow after the syrupy mouthful she'd just imbibed. "Now about Clay. I was wondering if you'd help me out."

He gave her an odd look. "Help you with Clayton Matthews?"

"Well, sort of. I want to have a party, a kind of housewarming. And I thought it would be fun to invite a group of people."

"Such as?"

"Well, Maryann and Beth will already be here, after all, they live here now. And Amy, and Beth's sister Ronnie. It can be their housewarming, too. And I want to invite Clay because he's my friend." She opened her eyes wide and refused to look guilty. "He is!"

"Uh-huh."

"And Garrett and Beth always used to get along."

"How about Peter…"

"No!" she wailed and then realized how strange that sounded. "Uh, maybe next time, Jordan. I don't want too many people around. Especially with me in this condition, I mean." Her cheeks heated when he met her gaze and held it.

"And these other 'friends' aren't going to wear you out? But Peter will." He raised one eyebrow. "Clear as mud, Lyn."

"It's just a little open house. People do that, you know." She ignored the knowing look in his eyes.

"Hmm. Isn't it odd that you've got them all paired off?" When she wouldn't meet his gaze, he sighed loudly. "All right. What do you want me to do?"

"Play host."

"I don't know Garrett or Clayton that well, Lyn. And your roommates I see only occasionally." He tilted his head to one side, his glasses drooping to the end of his nose and he peered over them. "I get it. You're matchmaking, right?"

"Not really." She shrugged when one arrogant eyebrow arched even higher. "I'm not! I just want them to get together and talk. Then maybe they can see how much the other has changed, that this isn't high school. Maybe they can forget the mistakes of the past."

"Let bygones be bygones, start afresh." He groaned, putting his cup on the table with a thud. "I know I'm going to regret this."

"No, you're not. It's just a social evening, Jordan. Nothing to get all excited about." She averted her head from his too perceptive stare. "I'll put on some music, we'll talk, it'll be great."

"Caitlin, these people have histories. I don't think they can just take up where they left off and develop a lifelong love, or they would have done it already."

He rose, walked around the table and sank down onto his haunches in front of her, one hand clasping hers.

"We've changed, all of us. You and I included. Time and distance does that to people. Affections change, too."

She stared down at him, wondering at the stain of red on his cheekbones. Did that mean he didn't care for her at all? Of course, he never had, had he? It had been her schoolgirl crush, all those years ago. Jordan had escaped as quickly as he could by dumping her on Michael.

Caitlin came back to the present with a jerk when Jordan, now flushed and discomfited, got up rather quickly and flopped back into his chair.

"What I'm trying to say is that the love they once felt, or that you think they felt, might be gone forever."

"It hasn't." She refused to believe that, not after talking to Beth and Maryann. There was something there, some spark that just needed a little nurturing. They deserved to find happiness.

"Okay. Nobody can say I didn't try." He raked a hand through his hair, mussing it worse than usual. "But you're not to go to a bunch of fuss. I'll get Mom to make some punch and I'll buy some chips and stuff."

"No." Caitlin swallowed down her dismay, trying not to let him see that she didn't want Eliza involved in such delicate matters of the heart. "I'll buy some of those frozen hors d'oeuvres or something so there's not a lot of work. I want to make my housewarming an occasion to remember.''

''I'm pretty sure it will be that.'' His forehead pleated. ''But fair warning. You may not want to remember it when those four see each other here.'' He shook his head. ''You may wish you'd left them alone to get on with their lives.''

''I won't.''

Jordan knew she was up to something. Caitlin could see it in his face. Too bad. She was going to do this, with or without him. It would just be a little simpler if she had him there. It would be nice to have him there to lean on.

''Thank you, Jordan,'' she murmured. ''I appreciate your help. With everything.''

''Don't be silly.'' His voice was brusque with gruff courtesy. ''I haven't done anything. Yet. And you may regret asking me to help out, you know.'' He held up a hand before she could get the words out. ''I know. Don't tell my mother.'' He sighed heavily. ''Fine.''

''Thank you, Jordan. You're a peach!'' She grinned at him, thrilled that he didn't even attempt to argue.

''A peach? First my own family tells me I'm fat, and now you call me a peach.'' He shook his head in disgust. ''Wonderful. Just wonderful.''

Caitlin giggled. ''No, really. I mean it. I appreciate this.''

His eyes narrowed. ''Good grief, Lyn, I'm not going to have to dance with him. Am I?''

She giggled, the very idea conjuring up a myriad

of hilarious scenes in her head. "I don't think so. I wasn't planning on including dancing."

"Good. Those big boots of his could be mighty uncomfortable on my delicate toes."

She felt his questioning glance study her more closely, searching for an answer to a question he didn't ask.

"Take it easy tomorrow. I'll come round after church and see if you need anything." He paused, his face tight with tension, as if something was bothering him.

"Really, Jordan," Caitlin protested, hoping her words would deter him from asking yet again. "That isn't necessary. I'll be fine. I just need a good night's sleep."

"I don't suppose you'd consider coming with me? Sing some hymns, hear the message, that sort of thing?" His voice was softly pleading.

She saw the glint of gold flash in those dark eyes as he studied her. Then he bent his head, one curling lock of hair falling over his brow.

"Right," was all he said, but Caitlin knew he got the point. She wasn't going to church tomorrow or anytime soon. She knew that Jordan would insist on coming over after, though.

"I'll see you in the morning then." He got up from the sofa and snatched his coat from the chair where he'd thrown it. "Try to get some rest, okay?"

She nodded. "I will. Thanks."

"Stop thanking me," he grumbled, preceding her

to the door. "I'll start to wonder if there's something else wrong with me."

"There is." She giggled. "But we'll save that for some other time, when you're feeling tougher."

He shook his head, rolling his eyes to the ceiling. Then, before she realized what was happening, Jordan leaned down and brushed her cheek with his lips.

"Good night, Lyn."

"Good night, Jordan." She watched him drive away before she closed the door and wandered back inside her cozy apartment.

In a way she was relieved he kept dropping in. It was so nice to have Jordan around, taking care of her, managing some of the things she was just plain too tired to deal with. Besides, his company was restful and interesting at the same time.

Although it would never do to admit to it.

Neither would it do to question too closely her pleasure in having him around. Certain things were best not probed too deeply.

Especially the rush of pleasure she'd felt when he'd kissed her, innocent though the embrace was. Strangely enough, she wished he'd held her.

Why, when she was demanding to stand on her own, did she feel bereft whenever Jordan Andrews left her home?

Chapter Seven

"**P**regnancy and housecleaning do not go together." Caitlin surveyed the newly acquired gleam of her bathroom with a grimace. "But Junior, you've got to admit, this place is spotless."

Her first week of maternity leave and she was cleaning the bathroom. It hadn't been easy. The bathtub looked fairly routine, but at this stage in the maternal journey nothing was simple anymore. The sheer width of her body made cleaning in the crevices an arduous task at best, but she finished anyway. For some reason, a clean bathroom seemed important today.

As she rinsed off her rubber gloves and stored them in the caddy under the sink, one hand slipped round her hips to rub a tender spot. It wasn't a new ache. It had been paining her for days. Deliberately Caitlin turned away from her reflection in the full-length mirror, refusing to acknowledge it or her sore back.

"I'm fine, this is normal. I'm perfectly healthy and nothing is going to go wrong. Right, Junior?" She patted her stomach with a smile and got a swift kick of reassurance. "Right."

She wandered down the hall to glance once more at the baby's room. It stood waiting in the late-afternoon shadows, ready to welcome its new inhabitant. In the corner, the dresser was stuffed with tiny clothes Jordan's mother had either made or purchased over the past week. Eliza sent the various items with Jordan on his daily visit to boss her around.

She bent down to check the mural, then straightened in relief. No, there wasn't a snake there. Yet. She wondered how long it would be before he tried to sneak in that, or the boat Jordan continually insisted on discussing.

While Caitlin had her doubts about the durability of tiny crocheted sleepers or paper-thin booties, she couldn't bring herself to say anything that would dampen the joy Eliza obviously found in getting these things for her grandchild. And Caitlin appreciated the gestures of love Michael's mother had made toward her.

Her eyes roved appreciatively across the mural once more. Jordan had done a very good job. It was a lovely room to welcome a new baby, even without the extras he wanted to add.

The doorbell rang and Caitlin walked to the top of the stairs. "Come in," she called, refusing to traverse the length of those steps again today.

"Caitlin, honey, it's me," Eliza Andrews called.

After a moment she caught sight of her daughter-in-law. "I brought something for the baby's room. I hope you're feeling okay." Her voice dropped in concern. "I'm not bothering you?"

Caitlin felt a hint of frustration. Everyone treated her with kid gloves these days. As if she'd break.

"Come on up," she called. "I'm on strike. I refuse to navigate those stairs again just now."

Eliza joined her, thrusting a flat square box into her hands. "This is for you and the baby, Caitlin."

"Thank you, Eliza. You're going to have to quit this, you know." Eliza's wistful smile aroused Caitlin's curiosity.

"This is one thing I had to bring."

"Come and see the nursery," Caitlin invited, moving down the hall. Although she had contributed a number of items to the baby's room, Eliza hadn't yet been in it and suddenly Caitlin had an urge to show off her and Jordan's handiwork.

She left Eliza to look around while she sank into the rocking chair and unwrapped the box. Eliza's gift was the finishing touch to an already perfect nursery. Nestled inside the foil package was a delicately embroidered ivory shawl. Caitlin shook it out carefully, then spread it across the rungs of the crib, ready to welcome its new owner.

"It's beautiful," she whispered, trailing one finger over the intricate design.

"It was Michael's," Eliza told her, smiling softly in remembrance. "His grandmother made it for him and when he was through with it, I tucked it away. I thought he might use it himself some day. For his own child.''

"It's perfect. Thank you, Eliza. The baby will love it." Caitlin patted her soft hand.

"It's not that I'm trying to keep Michael alive or anything, Caitlin," the older woman apologized, her eyes solemn. "I know he's in heaven and happy. That's the one thing that makes his death bearable. But I thought someday the baby might want some history of his father's, some link with the past. If you don't think it's a good idea, I'll understand. I know you have to get on with your life."

"I am getting on with life. And this is a wonderful idea! Thank you for thinking of it. To me, Michael will always be alive in here." Caitlin patted her heart. Her voice was full of tears and before long they were weeping all over each other. They didn't even hear Jordan arrive.

"What's all the bawling for?" he demanded, relief in his eyes at the sight of his mother cradling Caitlin's dark head. "I thought having a baby is supposed to be a happy occasion. You two look like you're in serious pain."

Eliza met Caitlin's raised eyebrows with a grin. "Son," she told Jordan affectionately, patting his broad shoulder, "women do not *bawl*. And these were tears of joy. I sincerely hope you're around when Caitlin goes into labor. Then perhaps you'll understand that children bring both joy and pain."

Her blue eyes twinkled merrily, winking at Caitlin

before they returned to her big, boisterous son. "In fact, some children bring more of one than the other."

Caitlin giggled at the frown that crossed Jordan's usually smiling face.

"Mother, I hope you aren't insinuating that I have ever been anything but the wonderful, loving, caring, obedient son you have always told me I am."

"Obedient, he says. As if he would ever listen to his parents?" Eliza's snort was an audible guffaw in the quiet house. Her tears vanished as she looked to Caitlin for support.

Jordan raised his eyebrows in shock. "As if I would ever go against your wishes. Mother, please!"

"Enough, you two." Caitlin held up a hand. "You'll set a bad example for my baby. He's going to be the sweetest, most amenable child there ever was. Just like his mother."

Jordan coughed. "And if that isn't a bit of make-believe, I don't know what is." He offered a hand up to Caitlin. "Come on, little mama. We're going out for your walk. Then supper."

Caitlin groaned, her green eyes beseeching Eliza to support her. "It's too icy outside, Jordan. And too cold. I just want to stay home tonight. Take your mother out, for a change. She'd enjoy it."

But Eliza shook her head in an emphatic "no." "Thanks anyway, Caitlin. I'll go home to Stan." She picked up her coat and slipped it on then led the way to the outside door, stopping only long enough to slip on her snow boots.

Caitlin held open the door. "Thank you for the

shawl, Eliza. I will treasure it. Be careful on the roads,'' she added, noticing the icy slickness of the driveway. She closed the door quickly behind her mother-in-law, shivering at the blast of cold air.

"I am not going out in that, Jordan. And I don't care what you say," she informed him, swishing around him and into the kitchen.

The cupboards weren't quite bare, but it was close. Caitlin stared at the lonely can of tomato soup and shrugged. It would do. At least it was better than chancing her footing on all that ice.

"We can have soup and toast," she told him firmly as he entered the kitchen. "That's nutritious and filling."

"It's not tomato soup is it?" he asked warily, glancing around her shoulder to peer at the label. "I knew it." His voice was full of defeat.

"What's wrong with tomato soup?" she demanded, whirling around to study him.

"Nothing," he muttered.

"It's just that I ate it almost every day for a solid year when I was going to college," he told her. "I had to save my money to take this girl out, so I lived on soup. I got a great deal on a case of tomato."

He ignored her snicker.

"I made a vow that when I graduated and started work, I would never eat the stuff again unless there was nothing else." He yanked open a cupboard door and stared at the empty shelf.

"Well, it looks like that time has arrived!" Caitlin

grinned. "But that's okay. I love tomato soup. You can have toast."

"Caitlin!" Jordan let out an exasperated sigh. "How can you not have any groceries in the house? You're supposed to be eating healthfully and there's nothing in this fridge but a dried-up bit of lettuce."

"If you recall," she said matter-of-factly, stirring the thickening soup steadily, "these past weeks you have taken me out almost every single night for dinner. I hardly need groceries."

"Ridiculous," he replied, slamming the door closed and snatching up his heavy leather jacket from its usual position on her easy chair.

"Where are you going?" She pointed to the toaster. "Your supper is almost ready."

"That isn't a meal," he told her. "That's a bedtime snack. I'm going shopping and if you're nice, I'll bring some goodies back." His eyes glinted behind his glasses. "If there was a snowstorm, you'd starve to death here. Honestly woman, how can you be so careless of yourself?"

His chastising tone hurt. Caitlin felt a wave of misery close over her and seconds later heard herself burst into tears which made her even more disconsolate.

"I am not careless," she said. "I simply hate lugging those heavy bags back from the store and since I can't drive, I have to use the bus."

"I'm sorry, Lyn," he said at last, using his handkerchief to wipe the tears off her cheeks. His voice was soft and full of concern. "I never even thought of that or I would have taken you there myself. Just stop crying now, okay?''

"I am *not* c-c-crying,'' she blubbered, his gentleness affecting her more than his anger had. "I never cry!''

Jordan tugged her into his arms and held her as she sobbed miserably on his shoulder.

"Of course you're not,'' he murmured, a wry grin tipping his lips. "Any fool can see that. You merely have a leak in your eyes that allows moisture to fall out in huge droplets that roll down your cheeks and soak my shirt. Obviously not crying! How stupid of me.''

She pushed out of his arms, embarrassed by the whole thing. Turning her back to him, Caitlin filled the kettle and put it on to heat, striving for a tiny measure of control when her nerves screamed frustration.

"Caitlin?'' He turned her around and slid one finger under her chin, tipping her tearstained face up toward his. "Just make a list and I'll pick up whatever you need, okay?''

"I don't need someone to look after me,'' she bristled angrily. "I'm not a child that needs a keeper.''

She heard the sigh. Anyone would have. It was loud and forbearing as if there were thousands of things he *could* have said, and yet nothing he was willing to verbalize.

Guilt, frustration and tiredness welled up inside, each one vying for supremacy. She was fed up with figuring out which one was worse. All she wanted to do was give in to this need to cry.

Why couldn't everyone just leave her alone? She'd get through this. Somehow. In her own way.

"Just for right now, just tonight, let me be my brother's keeper, okay?" His gentle fingers turned her to face him, his golden eyes beseeching her. "Actually, that should be my sister-in-law's keeper."

"I promise, it will just be tonight." That tender note in his voice was her undoing.

Caitlin couldn't ignore him. "This one time you can help me out," she agreed finally. "Is it a deal?"

"Scout's honor." He held up one hand with two fingers pointing upward. "I promise I will never help you again. Not even if you beg me on bended knee. Now will you give me that list?"

"I could go myself," she told him, frowning. "I'm kind of picky about what fruit and vegetables I eat."

"Do you really want to go parading around a supermarket, pushing past people, standing in line and lugging everything across an icy parking lot to the car? I'm not going to take over your life, Caitlin. I'm just trying to help out."

"You have already *helped* me," she told him seriously. "It's not that I'm ungrateful Jordan. It's just that I have to learn to depend on myself. I have to manage on my own. I can't expect people to come running every time the Widow Andrews needs something." She peered up at him, trying to make him understand.

"I'm a grown woman, Jordan. I have to be able to

handle things as they come up. I have to be sure that
I can manage it all." She smiled tiredly. "I know you
think I'm obsessing about Michael, but I'm not. I understand that we're all human, that death is a part of
life. That simply means you have to be strong enough
to take it. Right now there is only me for my baby.
He's depending on me and I have to learn to be self-
reliant."

She waited, watching his eyes darken and narrow
as he absorbed what she'd said. When he spoke his
voice seemed leashed, held back.

"Yes, Lyn, people die. But can't you understand
that while they're here, a lot of them just want to do
what they can to make your life a little easier? Can't
you see that it hurts us to see you struggling on your
own when it's so easy for us to lend a hand?"

His face was serious, carved in lines of concern as
he stared down at her. "We're not asking for anything
from you, Caitlin. My parents don't expect anything
from you. They just want to be there because you're
their daughter-in-law and they love you. My sisters
just want their friend back in their lives."

Caitlin squinted up at him through the mist of tears
that seemed to constantly block her vision these days.
She remembered how many times in the past week
she'd put Robyn and her sisters off, pretending she
was too busy to see them, have lunch, talk.

"Can't you accept just a little bit of that love,
Lyn?"

It was a persuasive argument and she felt so alone.
Caitlin stared at the table in front of her and admitted

to herself that she did want to be part of their group again. She wanted to rejoin the human race, but on her own conditions.

"It's just that I have nothing to give them back," she whispered at last, sinking into a nearby chair.

"I'm empty, Jordan." She met his softened gaze. "Sometimes I think the last part of me that is capable of love only lives because of this baby."

He squatted in front of her, placing his hands on either side of her as his velvety soft gaze stared straight into hers. "Then just relax and let us fill the empty space. We'll do the work." He smiled softly. "All you have to do is accept it. That's all we ask."

One hand reached up to smooth her hair away from her tired face. "It's sort of like that with God, too. When we think we can't go another step, He's there to lean on and support us until we can catch our breath, gather our resources and continue with the journey." Jordan stood abruptly and zipped his jacket closed. His hand reached out and swiped the list from her fridge.

"For once in your life, Lyn, let someone else be in control. Just sit back and enjoy the ride." He grinned down at her. "I'll be back in a while. With real food."

Ten minutes later, as she sat sipping the tomato soup and munching on a square of toast, Caitlin thought about his words. Just like God, he'd said. Well, she didn't know much about God.

Oh, she had gone to church all her life and she was familiar with the hymns and choruses one sang in church. But she had never really thought of God as someone who was there to lean on. He'd always seemed an authority figure, somewhere way out there, sort of awesome and fear inducing. But the way Jordan spoke, God was like a person.

Caitlin leaned back in her chair and considered that. To be able to relax and let someone else shoulder the worry, that would be something. Not to feel guilty if she just gave in and believed that someone else would figure things out, to just go with what felt right to do today and not constantly worry about the future.

Of course, it wouldn't work for her. She had to plan each facet of her life. She had to make sure there were no surprises, she had to be prepared for anything life threw at her. Because if she wasn't, she would be hurt and abandoned just as she had been in the past. And she couldn't take that. Not again.

Caitlin cleaned up the kitchen and carried her tea into the living room, in front of the fire. A feeling of dread fell upon her as each moment ticked past on the old grandfather clock in the corner. What was taking Jordan so long?

He'd been gone for over an hour now. And the most recent check out the window had shown signs of a prairie storm blowing in. Everything was white, swirling snow. Caitlin could barely see to the end of the drive and as she peered out, her mind noted that the few cars that were out had to pass through the white drifts covering the road.

The phone peeled its urgent summons, causing her to jump.

"Yes," she murmured nervously, a trill of anticipation rolling down her spine. But the caller had a wrong number.

Please God, if you're there, don't let anything happen to Jordan.

She spent a long time saying that over and over, her television program long since forgotten. Caitlin was just adding another log on the fire when Jordan burst through the door carrying bags and bags of groceries. Arms loaded, he shoved the door closed with his foot.

"What in the world did you buy?" she demanded, aghast at the amount of the bill she found in the first sack. "I live alone, Jordan."

He grinned down at her. "But you're eating for two, right?" He hung his damp coat on the doorknob and picked up several sacks, lugging them through to the kitchen. "Come on, woman. You need to get this stuff put away."

But Caitlin was already sorting through the first bag. "Triple-chocolate-almond-pistachio ice cream?" she asked, one eyebrow raised enquiringly.

"It's my favorite," he told her grinning. "I knew you'd want to have something special to serve me when I come to visit."

Caitlin stared at him. "And the dill pickles?" she asked solemnly.

"Oh, those are for you. You know, pickles and ice cream. It's apparently all the rage with pregnant women." When she made a face he pulled out a package of freshly ground coffee and held it up. "Also for you, milady."

Caitlin sniffed as the fragrant aroma wafted across the room. She closed her eyes at the wondrous essence of her favorite blend. He was at her side in a moment.

"Lyn, are you all right?"

"Perfectly," she whispered reverently. "I'm just enjoying the full-bodied zest of something other than herbal tea. Junior may stop me from drinking the stuff but even he can't object to my merely smelling it." She opened her eyes to find him grinning down at her. "It is not funny." She raised her eyebrows.

"It's hilarious," he returned solemnly, his velvet eyes caressing her. "How the mighty coffee drinkers have fallen. And by a tiny little baby!"

"That's not very nice," she mumbled, slicing a teeny piece off the gigantic slab of cheddar cheese he'd purchased. "I've never made fun of you for your little quirks. And you do have a lot of them, don't you?"

He only ignored her teasing verbal jabs and continued to lug in bags and packages from the entry.

"Grade A extra-large eggs, fresh whole milk, cream for my coffee, grapefruit, oranges, Granny Smith apples. Although why you want to eat anything so sour I can't imagine. They do nothing for your disposition." He held up a hand when she would have protested.

"Cantaloupe, lettuce, tomatoes, celery, a turkey..."

"A turkey?" Caitlin stared at him. "Are you crazy? I can't eat a whole turkey, it will go to waste. Jordan, really, this is too much."

He ignored her, stuffing groceries into her cupboards and fridge like a grocery store shelf-stocker intent on completing his job in record time.

"Jordan, will you listen to me?" Caitlin tugged on his sleeve, forcing him to abandon the jumbo box of rice cereal he was trying to juggle into a cupboard that was just too small.

"Jordan!"

"Yes, dear." He sounded like some wife-weary husband who added the appropriate comments but heard nothing that was said.

"Would you please stop that and listen to me?" He turned a blithe, unconcerned face toward her. "I cannot possibly eat a whole entire turkey myself. You'll have to take it back."

"In this snow?" He shook his dark head. "I don't think so. You can invite somebody over or something, couldn't you? Like me?" There was a twinkle in his eyes that should have alerted her.

"Not even you with your gigantic appetite could eat this thing," she muttered, poking the frozen bird with one finger. "It doesn't seem in very good condition, either." Caitlin pointed to the torn packaging in the inner covering.

"Oh, I had it sawed into four pieces," he told her smugly. "That way you can have four smaller meals instead of one big one and it will still be fresh. I'll roast some for you if you like."

Caitlin held the freezer door open for him and shoved the ice cream out of the way as she groaned. "Oh, no. Not in my kitchen. No way. I've seen you cook Jordan. It is *not* a pretty sight."

He chucked her chin with his forefinger as his dark head shook sadly. "Oh, ye of little faith. I'm a wonderful cook. I can cook the socks off my mother, if you want to know. You're going to be sorry."

"Oh, no I'm not," she retorted smartly. "I've seen the kitchen when you've finished one of your so-called specials." Caitlin raised her eyebrows scornfully. "I can't afford to hire cleaners for the next month. The last time you cooked, your mother said it took three weeks to get the spaghetti sauce off the ceiling. And I saw the pot you forgot to turn off." She shook her head. "Uh-uh. No way."

He smacked the bags together smartly and stuffed them into a drawer with resignation. "Fine, if that's the way you want to be."

"It is," she assured him, grinning as she bit into another piece of cheese. "I like the simple things— clean cupboards, shiny floor, laundry done. You know, the normal stuff."

"Anybody can be normal," he muttered. "It takes talent to make something really spectacular. Hey!" His face brightened. "You've never had my black forest cake, have you?"

"Down, Jordan. It's too late to start baking now. Did you have something to eat already or would you like a sandwich? For some odd reason there's a package of corned beef here. I hate corned beef. Too fatty.''

He smiled from ear to ear. ''That's just your professional nutritionist side talking. I had some at the store, samples you know. It really is very good. Especially with sauerkraut.'' He watched her shudder. ''Some people have no taste,'' he complained sadly.

''That's for sure.'' Caitlin handed him a check, stuffing it in his shirt pocket when he didn't immediately take it.

''Thank you very much, Jordan. I really appreciate all of it. Are you sure you don't want to take some home with you?'' she asked, holding the deli bag with his corned beef daintily between two fingers.

''Naw,'' he grinned smugly. ''Keep it for the next time I visit. Instead of tomato soup. I didn't buy any of *that*.''

''I noticed.'' Caitlin longingly eyed the succulent golden-brown butter tarts he'd purchased. They were large and oozing with calorie-laden sweetness.

''Let's see,'' she murmured, mentally adding up the calories. ''If I just had one slice of toast...''

''I'm leaving,'' he interrupted her. ''I think I'd better get going before I have to shovel my way home.'' His eyes narrowed as he watched her pick the tarts up and then put them down. ''Why don't you just eat one if you want it?'' he muttered curiously, when she finally slid the package into the cupboard and closed the door firmly.

''I've already overindulged with the cheese,'' she

told him. "I can't have one of those, too. Besides, too much fat. I have enough already."

"You're not fat. You're pregnant." Jordan laughed at her as he studied her rounded figure. "Besides, you'll lose it all when the baby comes."

"I wish." Caitlin turned her mouth up. "A twenty-five-pound baby would be just a little big, don't you think? No, as it is I'm going to have a tough row to hoe to get back into my clothes after Junior shows up." She turned her back resolutely on the tempting bits of pastry sheltered behind the oak door. "I can't afford that."

"Can I have one for the road, then?" he asked grinning. "I need to keep up my energy." When she waved at the cupboard, Jordan helped himself to two of the confections. "It's really, really cold out," he told her wide-eyed stare.

Caitlin giggled and wrapped two more of the tarts in a napkin, then followed him through the living room.

"Thanks again," she said as he shrugged into his jacket. "I appreciate it."

The snow had blown up against the house when she tugged open the door. A little pile fell inside.

"See you tomorrow," he murmured, brushing a hand across her hair.

"Don't bother," she told him firmly. "It might be too slippery. I'll stay indoors and have a lazy day. I'll be fine. Good night, Jordan," she said when it seemed he would argue.

"Good night, little mama. Sleep well." Then he was gone.

"Sleep," she muttered to herself as she wandered back into the kitchen. But it was no use. She couldn't ignore the tarts.

Ten minutes later Caitlin sank into the big armchair in her living room with a pot of tea and a tart nearby, the television turned on low.

"As if I could sleep with those things calling my name. I don't know why he wanted a list. He replaced tofu with turkey, low-fat cottage cheese with cheddar, and turnips with tarts."

Caitlin closed her eyes and sank her teeth into the creamy smooth sweetness, letting it fill her mouth with that delectable taste.

"Do lots of push-ups, Junior," she ordered. "You and I are off turnips for the next few days and we need all the calorie burn we can get."

Caitlin tugged her notepad closer, ignored the pastry crumbs dotting her shirt and set about planning her housewarming party. It would be a quiet evening. A little conversation, a little food, maybe even some romance for her friends.

What could go wrong?

Chapter Eight

"It's just an evening with some friends, Clayton. Nothing to worry about. Come on! We're waiting for you." Exasperated, Caitlin hung up the phone before the man could ask her the one question she'd avoided at all costs during the past week.

"He's not too thrilled about coming, is he?" Jordan's lip sloped up when she turned her head away. "Wants to know if Maryann is here, I'll wager." He laughed when Caitlin turned her back. "I thought so."

"What are you doing out here anyway?" she demanded, bending to check the tiny puff pastries in the oven. "You're supposed to be in there, keeping the conversation going!"

"Hah! What conversation? Gar, as I've been told to call him, sits there like a bump on a log, staring straight ahead. Beth is on the other end of the sofa, glaring at the fireplace. They won't even look at each other, let alone speak.''

''And Maryann?''

''Maryann went upstairs, ostensibly to check on her daughter.''

''What? You're not supposed to let her go up there!'' Caitlin whirled around, hands on her hips. ''Some host you turned out to be.'' With a flick of her wrist, she opened the oven, emptied the pan of shrimp hors d'oeuvres onto a plate and shoved them at him. ''Here.''

Obligingly, Jordan reached out and took one.

''They're good,'' he murmured in obvious surprise.

Caitlin sighed. Nothing was going right tonight.

''Of course they're good.'' She chuckled, whooshing a puff of air over her heated forehead. ''And they're supposed to be for *our guests,* the ones *you* are supposed to be serving.''

''Oh.'' He took the platter and moved toward the other room. ''How long do I have to stay in there this time?'' He looked like a little boy who had just been sent to his room.

''Until I come in and tell you otherwise. Now get them talking. You can do it, Jordan. You can talk about anything.''

A man forced to walk to his own execution couldn't have looked more pathetic. Caitlin grabbed the tray of glasses from the counter and headed in after him.

The scene before her was pathetic. The other two inhabitants refused to look at each other, deliberately focusing their sights on some faraway spot. Maryann eventually returned to the room and took her seat, glancing worriedly from one to the other of her friends. Jordan shoved the platter in front of each of them in turn and then almost dropped it when the doorbell rang.

"I'll get it," he called, rushing toward the entry in jubilant relief.

Caitlin frowned at his retreating back, drew a deep breath and plunged in.

"Beth, how's your sister enjoying school in Oakburn? Does she get into as much trouble as we did?"

"She loves it." Beth's voice warmed. "She a real clown and the drama teacher wants her to audition for the spring play."

"That's great! Remember how you and Gar played Romeo and Juliet...?" Maryann's voice died away, her face flushing painfully as she realized that she'd just linked the two of them when it was obvious neither wanted to remember the past.

Thankfully, Clay chose that moment to come through the door.

"Clayton! How lovely to see you." *At last,* Caitlin added under her breath. "Would you like some punch?"

"I'll get it," Jordan offered.

"I'll help him." Gar got up and sauntered away, his icy gaze almost freezing Beth out.

"I, uh, that is, I think I should go with them," Clayton blurted.

Caitlin could have groaned. This was exactly what

she hadn't wanted! Boys on one side, girls on the other. It was just like a junior high school dance. How could this matchmaking idea have gone so wrong?

When the doorbell rang again, Caitlin couldn't help rushing to answer it. The tension in her living room was thick enough to slice with a knife and she was at her wit's end.

"Please let it be someone who can help," she whispered and then realized that she'd just prayed to a God she wasn't speaking to. Who was she trying to fool anyway? She needed God in her life more than ever.

"Hi, sweetheart," Eliza said as she came inside. "Stan and I thought we'd drop over and see what you were doing. I saw Jordy's car here and figured you might like help." She peeked around the corner into the living room. "A party? Oh, honey, should we stay?"

Well, why not? Maybe Eliza and Stan could infuse a little warmth into the room. Caitlin certainly wasn't having much success.

"Of course! Come on in." She took their coats and hung them up, then ushered them into her living room. "What's that?" Caitlin motioned to the boxes under Stan's arm.

"Oh, he bought *more* games!" Eliza sighed heavily, but her eyes twinkled with love. "They're for four or more players so, naturally, we thought of you and Jordy."

Introductions were performed all around. Caitlin didn't know when or how it happened, but suddenly the room was filled with laughter. True, neither of the couples really looked at the other, and they sure weren't seated together. But it was a start, and it was far more fun than it had been.

The games Stan had picked up enlivened the evening immensely, especially the murder mystery. Two hours later they sat around sipping coffee and discussing it.

"I might have known I wouldn't guess." Beth giggled. " I never do and I love to read mysteries. But no matter how many I finish, the ending always comes as a complete surprise."

"Hey, Caitlin, you certainly picked the perpetrator out quickly. You and Jordan seem to have the same criminal mind-set." Stan cocked an inquisitive eyebrow. "Anything you want to tell us about?"

Six sets of eyes focused on them, a question mark in each one. Caitlin felt herself flush.

"You don't need to look at me as if I've robbed a bank of something! It was a perfectly logical assumption. The old man would have had longer to learn about toxins, wouldn't he?"

"Uh-huh." Maryann sipped her coffee slowly, eyes pensive. "And I suppose you know all about semiautomatic weapons and poisons, too. Right, Jordan?" She snickered. "Folks, we've got us a regular Bonnie and Clyde here!" She winked at the others.

"They know now, Lyn," Jordan boomed, dropping a casual arm around her shoulders. "That means we can start spending the loot we lifted from that last heist. What do you want to spend it on first?" His pinch on her waist told her to play along.

Well, she'd prove to him that Caitlin Andrews wasn't the dowdy old stick-in-the-mud he remembered from school.

"Oh, I don't know," she sighed, tapping a forefinger against her chin, fully aware of his hip pressed against hers on the crowded sofa. "It's all so difficult. Perhaps the tiara. Of course, they're very passé these days!"

His warmth and closeness were doing funny things to her blood pressure and she eased away from him on the pretense of checking the food. A few moments later she balanced on the arm of Stan's chair. Jordan noticed and frowned at her.

"Oh, a tiara is so boring." Maryann pooh-poohed the idea. "What else?"

"Then, of course, there is the villa. Spain's so lovely this time of year. You probably don't notice the cold as much as I do, Jordan, since you've just come back from the tropics."

And truthfully, it did feel cooler without his protective arm around her. But the atmosphere in this room, in her home was warm and friendly, exactly the way she'd always dreamed.

Caitlin let the others' conversations whirl around her while she thought about those dreams. She'd always wanted a real home, a refuge where she could feel safe and comfortable. Loved. Perhaps she'd finally found it? She glanced at the smiling faces, stopping on Jordan's longer than anyone else. What she saw in those golden eyes warmed her heart.

"Uh-oh! Caity's deep in a new intrigue!" Stan's voice finally penetrated her cloud of reminiscence, making her blush furiously.

"I was just telling them about the Lear." Jordan's voice took the focus off her. "Once I get the computer system revamped to my specialized form, we'll be ready to take off. And no one will be able to follow us."

He said it to the others, but his warm brown eyes were on her, a question in their depths.

"Why, sir!" she drawled, fluttering her fingers at him and adopting her best Southern accent. "I'm about to become a mother! I simply couldn't fly away just now. Tell me, are there mint juleps in Spain?"

Everyone burst into delighted laugher at her perfect imitation of Scarlett. There was even a small round of applause. Then Clay's low voice broke in.

"I have to go, Caitlin. I've got some sick animals at home and I need to watch them pretty carefully." He got to his feet. "I'll see you Monday night, right?"

Why did he have to make it sound like some sort of a date? Caitlin asked herself as she nodded, found his coat and escorted him to the door.

"Do you think she noticed the 'Monday night' part?" he whispered, pulling on his Stetson.

"Maryann?"

He nodded.

"I'm quite sure she couldn't have missed it," she

told him wryly. She sighed. This matchmaking thing was taking far more out of her than she had anticipated. By comparison, having a baby was child's play.

"Good. I don't want her to think I'm not attractive to other women." He stood staring down at her, his eyes roiling with emotion.

"I keep telling you that you're not unattractive," Caitlin grumbled. "You're just rusty. You need some practice. Why don't you ask Vivian Michaels out? She's a nice friendly girl."

"A little too friendly for my taste! I asked her out once a couple of years ago and she showed up at my house the next day with a cake."

"What's wrong with that? She was only trying to be friendly."

"Friendly? Hah!" His eyes glinted with anger. "She offered to cook my Christmas turkey." His face tightened into a mask of scandalized outrage. "I knew she was up to no good as soon as the words left her lips."

Caitlin choked down the laughter that burbled up inside with a gigantic effort. "Clay, Viv was probably just offering to help you fix Christmas dinner. She's alone a lot now, with her mother gone. She probably wanted someone to share some Christmas cheer with."

"She wanted to share a lot more than that," he insisted grumpily, shoving his arms into the sleeves. He zipped the coat closed with one motion. "Well,

I'd better go.'' He stared at her for a moment, then his eyes opened wide.

Caitlin half turned to see who had come into the hall, but she found her chin grasped. Her head jerked up just in time to receive a kiss that landed to the left of her mouth, close to her jaw. It was anything but loverlike.

"Oh, excuse me!" Maryann's breathless voice told Caitlin everything she needed to know. Her heart sank as she heard the sound of footsteps rushing up the stairs to the second floor.

"Why did you do that, Clayton Matthews?" Caitlin demanded hands on her hips, glaring at him. "Why in the world did you do that?"

"Exactly what I'd like to know."

Sometime in the disaster of the past few moments, Jordan had joined them in the foyer. He stood tall and menacing, his eyes chilly as he glanced from her to Clay.

"I can kiss a woman," Clay blurted, obviously completely disconcerted by the other man's presence.

"I'm not debating that. I just want to know why it's Caitlin you're kissing."

"She's my friend. I like Caitlin."

"And she likes you. That's why she's trying to help you with Maryann. You remember Maryann, don't you, the woman you're supposed to like? The one who just watched you kiss someone else?"

His scornful voice stung Caitlin. She could only imagine how poor Clay felt. He'd tried the only thing he could think of to make Maryann jealous. Unfortunately, it had backfired.

"I do like Maryann." But as Clay glanced uncertainly from Jordan's twitching jaw to the staircase, Caitlin knew he was second-guessing his hasty decision.

Repairs between the two men were up to her and Caitlin searched for the right words. "Clay, Maryann is already a little skittish where men are concerned. I don't think making her jealous is the right way to attract her attention. She was married to a man who abused her trust. She won't risk her heart again, especially not if she sees you kissing me. You'll have to find a way to apologize, you know."

"Yeah, I suppose you're right. Romance her, you said?" He sighed, chest heaving, face drooping at the thought. "You're sure it's the only way?" His look told her he was exceedingly skeptical.

"I think it's the *best* way."

Caitlin knew he wasn't too sure about that. But he didn't argue. Instead he shoved his feet into his number fourteen cowboy boots, hunched his shoulders and yanked the door open.

"Okay. Romance it is. I'll apologize tonight if she answers the phone. Sorry, Jordan. See you Monday, Caitlin."

"Yes, I'll see you then. And Clay?"

"Yeah?" He raised one eyebrow.

"Don't worry about it so much," she murmured, going on tiptoe to brush a friendly caress against his cheek. "Everything will work out just fine."

"That's what I'm praying for." He stood a moment, bemused by her touch, one hand rubbing the spot. "Course, I prayed for it ten years ago, too."

"Just keep at it, Clay. It will happen." Jordan closed the door on the man, then turned to Caitlin. His forehead was pleated in a frown.

"Why'd you kiss him?"

She hooked her arm through his and led him back into the living room, shivering as a tickle of warmth crawled up her spine. Jordan was jealous? Of Clay? The very idea was, well, exhilarating. She'd never had anyone be jealous of her before. It meant Jordan cared. Didn't it?

Beth walked over to them and smiled. "Thanks for a fun evening, Caitlin. But I've got to run. Night everyone."

"Good night, Beth," Caitlin said with a sigh as Beth walked out of Caitlin's apartment and across the hall.

"I've got to go, too," Garrett Winthrop's voice reminded Caitlin that neither of her schemes had worked out properly. "I'd like to talk to you sometime, Caitlin. Whenever you have a spare minute." There was a hint of authority there that told her he expected it to be soon.

Caitlin sighed. "I've started my maternity leave you know. I'm sure there will be lots of time before the baby arrives. Is next week okay?"

"It's fine. Nothing pressing. Just some things I need to know. For the bank." Gar bid the Andrewses good-night, then followed Jordan out of the room.

Caitlin sagged against her chair, flopping into it with relief.

"Sweetheart, you're dead on your feet!" Eliza's caring hands gently massaged her shoulders. "Thank goodness you're off now. You were taking on too much."

"I'm fine. Really. And I did have a good time tonight."

"It was fun, wasn't it?" Eliza looked around the room. "I remember this house from when the Cardmore sisters lived here. They loved to have tea parties, you know. We'd get all gussied up and come over for cucumber sandwiches and iced tea in the summer. They had the coolest house in town."

Caitlin nodded, trying to stifle a yawn as Eliza continued her story.

"That was before air-conditioning. How those two used to giggle and twitter."

Stan shook his head in remembrance and tugged at his wife's arm. "Come on, honey. Caity's falling asleep."

"Of course she is! The poor girl's been on her feet all day, I imagine. I'll just load those few dishes into the dishwasher and then we'll be off. You can help."

Caitlin chuckled at Stan's groan of agreement and watched as the older couple left the room. But she made no effort to hoist herself out of her chair. Instead she shifted her feet onto a footstool.

"Finally seeing the light?" Jordan strode across the room and sat down in a chair across from her.

"Pardon?" She knew exactly what was coming,

but Caitlin pretended ignorance. He didn't have to rub her face in her capitulation.

"You know what I'm talking about, Lyn." His dark eyes mocked her. "But I'm perfectly willing to play dumb if it means that you'll allow my family to help out once in a while."

She closed her eyes. "Don't bug me, Jordan. I'm too tired to argue with you tonight."

"You look beautiful." The softly spoken words jarred her from her dream. "Am I allowed to say that at least? I like that misty-green color on you. It makes your eyes stand out."

She snorted, glancing down at her stomach. "I look more like a pile of beached seaweed than anything wispy and you know it."

Caitlin fiddled with her skirt, unwilling to look at him. His words, his touch, even his presence made her nervous when he stopped acting like Michael's brother. She liked it, but it still made her nervous.

He sighed, exasperation evident in his body language. "I wish you could see what I see when you look in the mirror."

"I'm glad I can't." she said with a self-conscious laugh.

"You'd see a gorgeous woman who glows with life." He ignored her interruption. "Your skin has this luminous quality that the makeup companies would kill to emulate."

"That's because it's stretched so thin." She chuckled.

"Stop it! Stop decrying yourself. You're a beautiful woman, Lyn. Pregnancy has only added to that beauty.'' He stood up as his parents came back into the room, his voice changing as he asked them, ''All done?''

''Clean as a whistle. There's nothing left for this little mama to do but to climb into bed and get some sleep.'' Stan leaned down and patted Caitlin's cheek as if she were one of his daughters. ''Good night, Caity. Thanks for the party.''

''You're the one who made it a party.'' Caitlin smiled, accepting Jordan's helping hand as she hoisted herself from the sofa. ''Before your arrival, we were dying fast.''

''Why?'' Eliza's eyes glowed brightly with curiosity.

''Let's jut say she's not as good at matchmaking as she thought.'' Jordan, tongue in cheek, ushered his parents to the front door. He found their coats, helped them on and wished them both good-night.

''Matchmaking?'' Eliza's brow furrowed, then cleared. ''Of course! I'd forgotten all about that. I've been so busy with you two...well, anyway I forgot.''

''Good! I wish Caitlin would, too. You can't force these people to like one another simply because you think they should. They've got a history to get past.''

''Rather like you and Caitlin.'' Stan's quiet voice drew their attention. ''You two dated for a while, then broke up and Caity married Mike. Now here you are hosting parties together.''

''Jordan's just helping out till the baby comes.

That's all.'' Caitlin felt the heat burn her cheeks as Stan's glance met hers.

"I know." He smiled and squeezed her hand. "And I'm really glad he is. It just goes to show that God can work in any situation, if we leave it up to Him."

Caitlin wanted to stop him, to straighten out his obvious misconceptions, to get rid of that smug glint in his eye. But there was no time. Whatever Eliza and Jordan had been whispering about, they had not come to any agreement. Eliza's lips were stubbornly pursed together and Jordan, well Jordan seethed with something, though he cloaked it well.

"We'd like you to come to dinner tomorrow, Caitlin. After church. Jordan can pick you up for the early service. We'll all sit together."

"Mother, I told you..."

"I'm not sure I'm going," Caitlin prevaricated, glancing from one to the other as she handed out the gloves they'd left on the hall table. To Stan she passed the games.

"Good! Nine-thirty." Eliza thrust her arm through Stan's and hurried him out the door even though he was still juggling the games. "Thanks again. See you in the morning."

Caitlin tried to say something. But before the protest could form, Eliza snapped the outside door shut, leaving her and Jordan alone.

"I don't think..."

"You don't have to..."

Jordan shook his head and smiled. "Sorry. You go first."

"I was just going to say that you don't have to pick me up. I can get to church myself." She took off her shoes and padded back into the living room, toes scrunching into the thick pile. "What were you going to say?"

"Nothing." He followed her in, shutting the door behind him.

"Yes, you were. What were you and your mother arguing over?" She peered up at him curiously. "Was it about me?"

"In a way." His eyes avoided hers as he rearranged the cushions on the sofa. "But don't worry, I set her right."

"About what? What was she saying?" Caitlin shifted from one foot to the other impatiently. "Jordan?"

When at last he straightened, Jordan seemed to have recovered the calm good humor that was his trademark.

"She's got some silly ideas, that's all."

Caitlin frowned, and shook her head. "What are you talking about?"

Had she missed something? Maybe Michael's family were getting tired of having to care for "little Caity." Maybe they wanted her to go to church so they could foist her off on some other poor souls.

"Jordan, please. What is going on?" she pleaded, hating the knot of fear that twisted in her stomach.

He wouldn't leave now, would he? Not when she'd

begun to rely on his strength and capability? Not now, when she'd only started to realize how much she needed him in her life, not so much as a link with the past, but as a connection to the future?

"I can see the fear in your eyes, Caitlin. And you can just stop it. I'm not going anywhere. I'll be here for as long as you and the baby need me." His crooked smile tilted down at her as his big warm hands closed around her arms, holding her in that strong but protective way.

Relief swamped her, blessed, light-headed relief that she wouldn't be alone to face this highest of all trials. Jordan, dear, sweet, dependable Jordan would be there to lean on.

Caitlin ignored the little gremlins that giggled inside her head and told her that having him around was exactly what she *didn't* want. She'd be strong later, after the baby was born, when things were back to normal. That was the time to face life and the future alone, not now.

"Caitlin?"

She focused on the present and realized the same question still existed. "I'm okay. So what did your mother say?"

He sighed. A long, resigned whoosh of air that told her he didn't like saying the words, but that he wasn't willing to lie, either. That was Jordan. Truthful, no matter what.

"She thinks we make a good couple."

Caitlin didn't get it. She frowned lightly, tightening her fingers on his muscular arms. "I suppose we do.

After all, we were trying to host this silly party together. Unfortunately, no one but us seemed able to talk to each other.''

She stopped, searching his face as the silence stretched between them. There was something there, something that told her she'd misunderstood his meaning.

''Jordan?'' The word came out quietly, half fearful at the glow of quiet purpose in his eyes.

''She meant couple as in a pair. Together. You and I. More than friends.'' He held her gaze with his.

''Oh.''

Caitlin didn't get it, didn't understand what he was hinting at. Jordan *was* her friend. They laughed together, did things, had fun. That was all there was to it. Wasn't it?

''But I'm Michael's wife,'' she blurted out, trying to reconcile his words in her mind.

''You were. Michael's gone.''

''I know that.'' Caitlin stepped back, dropping her hand from his arms. No, she wouldn't go there now. ''It's late. I know you want to get going. I'll find your coat.''

She scurried out into the hallway, half afraid of the glow that glimmered deep within those golden eyes.

''Here it is. Good night, Jordan.'' She waited as he shrugged into the warm jacket, smiling warmly as she stepped forward to the door.

''Lyn?'' Jordan stopped her, his hand curving around her shoulder to stop her progress.

She turned back to him, wondering at the strange

look on his face. The rugged planes softened as his hands drew her closer. Before she could do anything, his head came down and Jordan Andrews kissed her as if he'd been waiting forever.

It was over in seconds, but Caitlin didn't pull away. She couldn't. She merely stood there, locked in the circle of his arms, and stared blankly at his beloved face.

His hand came up to brush away the soft curls that fell around her cheeks. One finger traced a line from her forehead down her nose, past her lips to her upraised chin.

"Clayton Matthews has no business kissing you." The words were barely audible.

Then Jordan tilted his head and kissed her again, a warm friendly kind of kiss that Caitlin wanted to go on and on.

She didn't know how it happened but moments later she was free and Jordan was standing in the open door.

"Good night, Lyn," he murmured, stepping backward onto the step. "Sweet dreams."

"Good night, Jordan," she whispered to the closed door.

Chapter Nine

"Are you sure you should be doing this?" Clay Matthews shuffled awkwardly across the floor and took Caitlin's hand. "I mean, Jordan didn't seem too thrilled that you were helping me out. When I mentioned Monday, his face got all tight."

"Well, too bad. Jordan Andrews doesn't control my life. Now concentrate, Clay. You're not dragging around a sack of oats, you're dancing with Maryann."

"Maryann's not as big around as you," he muttered, pushing her forward.

"Gee, thanks." Caitlin rolled her eyes. "Can't you pretend, just this once?"

"If I pretend too much, I'd be too nervous to do anything."

Sighing heavily, Caitlin let him go and found the nearest chair, thankful she'd worn her sneakers for this. Her back ached like fire.

"Maybe we'd better delve into that area a little

deeper, Clay. Why does Maryann make you so nervous?'' And how come I never make anyone nervous? Concerned maybe, protective yes, but nervous? Nah.

While Clay rambled, Caitlin fell to thinking about Jordan's strange kiss and subsequent actions. He'd acted as if nothing had changed when he arrived the next morning to take her to church. And the dinner at his parents had gone off without a hitch, or another one of those knee-melting kisses.

They were pals, best buds, friends. So why did she feel so aware when Jordan scooped her hair out from her coat collar? And what about the way he'd so solicitously seen to her every need? He'd done nothing unusual, nothing to get upset about, and yet, every time his knuckles brushed hers, Caitlin felt herself tensing.

She'd told him she didn't need him, that she could manage. And when he'd dropped her off, she'd insisted that she wanted to spend last evening alone, in front of the fire. So why had she expected him to come in and play checkers?

It was crazy, that's what it was. And she was silly for even thinking about him like that. They were just friends and that was the way she wanted it. Right?

''Caitlin?'' Clay's somber eyes peered down at her. ''Did you hear anything I told you about Maryann?''

A ruckus in the front hall saved her from admitting that she hadn't heard a single word he'd said. ''I'll just see who that is,'' she murmured, scurrying across the room as Jordan's boisterous laugh rang out.

He was in the front hall, teasing Beth about her new boots.

"I doubt if you'll even be able to cross the street after a good blizzard, if you wear those things," he scoffed, trailing one finger down the new shiny leather. "The heels are way too high."

"That's good." Maryann giggled. "That way she can dig them into the ice. Traction." She and Jordan exchanged a look that had him slapping a hand over his grinning mouth.

"Well, I think they're gorgeous," Beth sniffed. "Caitlin, tell me what you think of my new winter boots."

As Jordan and Maryann turned toward her, Caitlin bent to examine the pliable leather and avoid his scrutiny. It was stupid that she felt as if he might see through her, peer into her brain. He might figure out that she'd skipped dinner.

"They're lovely," she offered. "So stylish. They'll look elegant no matter what you wear. I just wish I could manage to look as gorgeous as you do."

"You could never fit into those boots," Clay remarked from behind. "Your feet are way too big."

Maryann groaned, her eyes rolling with disgust. "Nice, Clay. That will really make her feel good about herself."

"It's the truth!" Clay's face turned a deep, dark scarlet.

"Don't you know you're supposed to tell a woman how lovely she is? Especially a pregnant woman. Believe me, we already know all our faults." Maryann glared at him, but a spark of teasing twinkled at the back of her eyes.

"I didn't say she had faults." Clay tilted his head to one side in confusion. "Did I? I don't think so. I just said—"

"We know!" Maryann turned her back on him and smiled at Beth. "I really do like them, Beth. Especially those heels."

"And I'll take care of telling Lyn how good she looks." Jordan's voice rumbled in Caitlin's ear, barely loud enough for the others to hear.

"High heels wouldn't look good on you, Maryann. You're already tall—" Belatedly, Clay held his tongue, his eyes just catching the glimmer of hurt in Maryann's face.

Caitlin could have groaned when she noticed the other woman had on heels.

"Gee, thanks," Maryann muttered, her face tinged a dark pink. "I think I'll go before you offer any more of your sweet-talking compliments on my appearance."

She hurried up the stairs, stumbling as she turned too quickly and her heel caught in the carpet.

"See, that's what I mean." Clay jerked his thumb toward the departing woman. "She always dresses up way too much for this place. Why doesn't she just wear normal clothes instead of those expensive dresses and fancy things?"

A resounding slam echoed back downstairs. Caitlin sighed, wishing she'd never come out here. Clay had singlehandedly done more to set back his own cause with Maryann than she could ever manage to correct, even if she paid for professional dance lessons for him.

She saw Beth jerk her head at Jordan and his almost imperceptible nod. Moments later he had his arm around Clay's shoulders.

"Clay, you and I need to have a chat, a man-to-man discussion." He shepherded the other man into Caitlin's apartment and firmly grasped the door handle to close the door.

"Well, maybe some other time. Caitlin was teaching me to dance!"

Clay's plaintive voice made Caitlin smile. She watched him stick his foot in the space.

"I haven't got a lot of time to waste talking, you know, Jordan." He sounded frustrated.

Jordan nodded. "Believe me, pal, I know just how little time you have! And we won't waste a minute of it. Besides, Caitlin's supposed to be getting a manicure from Beth right about now. Isn't that right?" he said over his left shoulder to the woman who stood holding her much maligned boots.

"Yes. Right." Beth scooped up the box and moved toward her apartment door. "Come on, Caitlin. Let's get at it."

Caitlin frowned at her hands and the fingernails she'd trimmed, filed and polished only that afternoon. That bit of pampering had filled in one of the long, lonely hours of her second Monday off work, but she didn't want to go through it all over again tonight.

"But I just..." She felt her arm yanked and scurried behind Beth into the apartment. "I've already done my nails today," she complained when the door had closed behind them.

"Fine. Then we'll do them again. Or we'll have tea. Or play Scrabble. Whatever. Let's just give those two a few moments alone together."

"You mean Jordan and Clay? But why?" Caitlin stared at her old school friend in puzzlement.

"Because Jordan can tell that guy a few home truths that you, even with all your careful wording, would never be able to explain to Clay Matthews." She ushered Caitlin through her bright red-and-white living room to the kitchen she'd decorated in the same vibrant colors.

"I shouldn't have said that," she admitted. "It's not his fault. It's just too bad he grew up with six brothers and a mother too tired from running a farm and raising those boys to have any time left over to teach the social niceties," she grumbled.

"This looks really nice." Caitlin admired the other woman's panache in decorating. "My place is dull and boring beiges and greens. Nothing like this."

"Your place is perfectly beautiful," Beth staunchly defended. "I didn't have much money to work with after setting up the shop, so I made my statement another way. The paint wasn't much and the stencils really add something."

"I like it. Veronica's out?"

"My sister is making her millions baby-sitting for the entire town." Beth rolled her eyes. "She desperately wants some new *cool* clothes, and since I need her help in the shop in the afternoons, she's decided to baby-sit in the evenings. She's been great about everything, moving here, changing schools, making new friends.''

"That's good.'' Caitlin wished she had a sister to room with. It must be nice to have someone to talk to when you needed an ally, someone who would sympathize unconditionally.

"I noticed you in church yesterday.''

"Yes.'' Caitlin sighed. "Jordan and his mother wouldn't take no for an answer. In the end, I guess he was right. It felt nice to be back in the old place. I notice the organ hasn't changed.''

Beth giggled as she put on the kettle. "Isn't it awful? That squeak has been there for years and nobody seems inclined to get rid of it. Sort of makes it feel more like home though, doesn't it?''

"I guess.'' Caitlin shifted from the bar stool to a kitchen chair. "I don't know. The truth is, I feel a little strange sitting in that church. Sort of guilty.''

"Guilty?'' Beth sat down opposite her and frowned. "For heaven's sake, what have you got to feel guilty for?''

Caitlin liked the way Beth sat there, waiting for her to explain. No pressure, no pushiness. Just the honest interest of a friend.

"It's, well, kind of hard to explain.'' Caitlin fought down the urge to pretend there was nothing wrong.

Beth sat where she was, her eyes softly sympathetic.

"I've blamed God, you see,'' Caitlin murmured,

embarrassed at having to admit such a thing. "I couldn't understand why Michael had to die, not when He knew we were going to have a baby. It seems so callous, not something a caring God would do."

"Yes, I suppose it does." Beth twiddled her fingers, grinning when Caitlin's surprised eyes met hers. "Hey, I never said I was perfect. I've often wondered why I had to grow up in the home I did. I didn't cause my dad's problems, so why should Veronica and I have to pay for them?"

Other people questioned God? The very idea of it was so new to Caitlin that she simply stared at her friend in disbelief.

"I was really angry at Him for dumping me in such a situation and then abandoning me. I used to envy you, Caitlin."

"Me?" Caitlin gaped, thinking of her scared, lonely teens. "Why would anyone envy me?"

"Because you lived with your aunt in a calm, fight-free house. You had it all together. Nobody yelled at you or called you an idiot. You were smart. You didn't have to look out for anyone."

"I couldn't have," Caitlin admitted quietly. "It was hard enough watching out for myself. And I had nothing together. I still don't."

"Besides, your aunt was no smiling violet," Beth added. "You don't have to tell me. I learned that later. That's partly how I found the nerve to face up to the ruins of my life and move on."

She walked to the stove, poured the boiling water

into a brown earthenware pot and added two tea bags. "It's also how I found out God is bigger than anything I can lay before Him. I asked Him to show me what to do next when my marriage broke down and He led me up north. Even though we fought, I learned how much my husband loved me and I began to understand that God cared for me more than I could imagine."

She set two big mugs on the table, poured the tea, retrieved the cream and sugar for Caitlin and then sat down.

"Just because I made a whole bunch of mistakes with my life, just because everything wasn't a bed of roses, didn't mean God had dumped on me. Even though all my circumstances changed, my duty remained the same."

"Your duty?" Caitlin accepted the mug of tea and sipped carefully, trying to sort through what she was hearing. "What duty?"

"I should have explained better." Beth scrunched up her eyes and thought before starting again.

"You see, Caitlin, if I wanted God to show me His way, I had to make Him the king of my life. Once I did that I had to accept His authority. Nobody gets to question a king. He makes the decisions He does and His subjects deal with them." She passed a bag of chocolate cookies across the table.

"I needed to accept that my life was the way it was. Period. I couldn't change the past, I couldn't change the people. I could only move on, follow

God's leading. That was the biggest relief. It was all up to Him.'' She grinned.

''And so here you are.''

''Here I am, back where I started, thanks to you. Trying to do what God tells me, to follow His lead, even though I don't understand it. I just have to believe that His way is best. That's my duty.''

''Duty. Hmm.'' Caitlin thought that one over, before glancing up into her friend's bright gaze. ''What do you think my duty is, Beth?''

''Sweetie, I can't answer that. No one can. That's between you and God.''

''I was afraid you'd say that. It just makes things worse.'' Caitlin heaved a sigh and closed her eyes. ''God doesn't talk to me.''

''How do you know that? Maybe you're just not listening. I do know that you'll never find out if you don't spend time talking to Him. Believe me, I know it's hard! But we only go on making more mistakes without some heavenly direction.''

Beth's small delicate fingers, punctured by the thorns and rough stems of the flowers she handled, closed around Caitlin's.

''You have to let go of the anger and the worry and the frustration, Cait. I know it's hard to fathom, but God would never do anything to deliberately hurt us. We usually bring that on ourselves. We just have to learn from it and move on.''

''That's almost exactly what Jordan said,'' Caitlin murmured.

''And he's right. Jordan wants to help. He wants

to be there for you, to do whatever you want him to. He cares for you, Caitlin.''

''That's the hardest part of all,'' Caitlin whispered, relieved to have finally said it out loud. ''I can't care for Jordan. Not like I did for Michael, not the way I think he wants. I...it hurts too much.'' And even that wasn't the truth. Not all of it, at least.

''And you think he'll take off the same way everyone else did.'' Beth's voice was flat. ''I can't tell you he won't, Cait. Nobody can do that except God and He doesn't usually tell us His plans for the future.''

''So what do I do?''

''You let him be your friend. You let him share in the joy of the baby, let him be an uncle. And you leave the rest up to God. If He wants you to do something, He'll show you.''

''That's all?''

Beth grinned. ''Isn't that enough? Just take it one day, one step at a time. Jordan cares for you. Anyone can tell that by looking at his face, by watching him when he's watching you. But he's not Michael, honey. He's not going to rush you into anything. For now, I think it's enough for him to be there, helping you however he can. And you don't exactly repel him, you know.''

She didn't answer. She couldn't. She *wanted* Jordan nearby, wanted him to be there, wanted to count on him. She just didn't think she could risk loving him.

Caitlin shifted uncomfortably in her chair. She'd deal with apologizing to Maryann in the morning.

Somehow. "Do you think they're finished their man-to-man talk now?"

"I don't know. But they can take it elsewhere. You need your rest." Beth marched to the door, opened it and led Caitlin across the hall. "Pregnant women need less stress in their lives, not more," she said loudly.

"All anyone seems to want me to do is rest," Caitlin mourned. "It's very tiring."

"I know you're tired. Hang on a sec." Her friend planted her knuckles against the wood and rapped.

Beth heard only what she wanted to hear, Caitlin mused. Maybe she was like that, too. She ignored the harsher parts of life, tried to gloss them over, so she wouldn't have to face them.

"Sorry, Lyn. Clay and I can take this somewhere else." Jordan smiled easily, his golden eyes glowing behind the glasses. "You get some rest."

Clay ambled to the door behind him. They both looked like they were hiding something.

"I wish everyone would stop saying that. I don't want to rest, I want to help Clay learn to dance so he can ask Maryann out." She slapped her hands on her hips and glared at the three of them. "If that's all right with you?"

Beth shrugged, murmured good-night and retreated to her apartment. Clay shuffled from one foot to the other uncomfortably but didn't offer a word of protest when she urged him inside her place. Jordan followed, closing the door behind him as Caitlin started the music once more.

"We do not require an audience," she told him firmly.

"I know. I'll just watch, see if I can help old Clay out with his footwork." Jordan flopped down on the sofa, his smile wide and endearing. "I won't be in the way, I promise."

No matter how much she glared at him, Jordan didn't move. Caitlin felt uncomfortably self-conscious as she urged Clay to take the lead. He wasn't even trying.

"I'm not that old, you know," he blurted as he stood in the middle of the room. "I just can't seem to dance."

"Here, let me show you." Jordan slid his arm around Caitlin's waist, and wrapped his fingers around her hand. "You don't push her back and forth like a sack of potatoes, Clay. You glide to the music. You choose the path and she'll follow. See?"

Caitlin allowed herself to sway to the music, effortlessly following Jordan's lead. He was as sure-footed in dancing as he was in everything else and for once she appreciate his confidence. It was much nicer to dance with a man who knew where he was going.

The music was soft and dreamy. Caitlin closed her eyes and drifted as a plaintive saxophone drew the last few notes out, pretending she was young again, instead of the age she felt right now.

"You're a wonderful dancer," Jordan murmured, his mouth next to her ear. "You really get into the music."

Another tune started and he kept going, sweeping her out of her dowdy surroundings and into a magical place where everything was perfect. She could hear a waterfall and a bird twittered in the background. In her mind's eye she could see lush green grass and wildflowers swaying in the breeze.

"It's easy to dance when you have a good partner." Caitlin opened her eyes and transported herself back to reality. "But I'm supposed to be helping Clay." She glanced around, spying the other man who stood staring out the window.

"I know." Jordan let her go without another word, watching silently. "Ready to try again, Clay?"

"It's nice of you to try to help me, Caitlin," Clay muttered as he took her hand and started to move the way she'd instructed. "But I don't think there's much point. Even if I could master these steps and feel comfortable doing them, I wouldn't know what to say to her."

"Talk about anything," Caitlin encouraged. "There's no set subject you have to discuss."

Jordan smiled to himself. Lyn was getting a little frustrated with this particular pupil. He could see it in the crease at the corner of her mouth when she reminded the erstwhile lover that Maryann was a mortal woman who was perfectly capable of conversing on a number of subjects.

"Do you think she's beautiful?" he heard her say.

Clay snorted. "Of course she's beautiful. Anyone with eyes can see that."

"Then why don't you tell her so? You can compliment her on her eyes or her lovely hair or on what she's wearing.''

Jordan winced along with Caitlin when Clay's big foot covered hers for the umpteenth time. She should have worn steel-toed boots!

''Her hair always reminds me of Naida's,'' Clay was saying.

Jordan frowned, hoping Caitlin would pick up on that.

''That's nice. But I don't think you should necessarily compare her to another woman.'' Her foot avoided his just in time.

''Naida's a sheep,'' Jordan murmured and watched as her eyes, now focused on Clay's, widened in a stare of shock. She forgot the music completely, staring at him as if he had just sprouted horns.

''You can't compare Maryann's hair to sheep's wool!'' Shock rendered her incapable of dancing and Caitlin stood where she was, her mouth an O of astonishment.

''But I like sheep's wool,'' Clay insisted. ''It's so soft. And the oil on it is really good for chapped skin.''

Jordan held his breath, choking down the laugh that burbled inside as he caught sight of Caitlin's stricken face. Her mouth opened and closed several times as she sought for the right words, but evidently there were none. She flopped into her chair with an air of utter futility, her eyes begging him for help.

Jordan got to his feet, wondering how he'd landed himself in this fix. The only person he'd even consider playing Cupid for was Caitlin. He just couldn't bring himself to ignore the mute desperation in her eyes.

He'd help her. After all, that was his role now, wasn't it? Big brother, uncle? He'd told her he was there for her whenever she needed him. Well, Caitlin Andrews needed him now.

"Clay," he sighed, motioning the other man to the remaining chair. "It's not a good idea to compare women, especially one you care about, to animals. Not in that way. If you want to talk about your animals, that's fine. But if you like her hair, just tell her that. You don't have to pretend to be something you're not."

Ha, his conscience jabbed him. Wasn't that exactly what he was doing right now, with his brother's wife? He was pretending to be her good friend, the brother-in-law who only wanted to help.

Well, he wanted a whole lot more than that! And if he told the truth, he always had. Shock reverberated through his system as the knowledge he'd deliberately hidden burst forth into the light.

Vaguely Jordan realized with some part of his mind, that Lyn and Clay were talking about goatskins. But he couldn't deal with that now. The truth that erupted inside his mind took his complete and total concentration.

He loved her! He always had. Even when he'd been so busy playing chivalrous big brother, he'd been in love with Caitlin. So why had he stood aside for Michael?

The answer was hard to accept.

Michael was young. He'd lived life to the max and he didn't worry too much about the future. Caitlin, in her shy, protected world, had gravitated to that like a bee to honey. He'd seen it himself the first time he'd introduced them. She'd been enthralled by Michael's shining light, riveted by his boyish joie de vivre.

By contrast, Jordan felt old and boring. And he was! He was older than both of them. He didn't want to speed around in fast cars or go to exciting parties. He didn't have to search for a vocation. He'd always known he'd be in computers. The same way he'd always known Caitlin would come back to him.

Of course, he hadn't expected Michael to marry her! That had come as a total shock. And a revelation. Jordan came home after the wedding, of course. He had to, had to see it to believe it. He'd even been coerced into playing a part in the celebrations his parents had thrown. But as soon as he could, he'd left, using business as his excuse.

Because even though Caitlin was married to Michael, Jordan still loved her. It was despicable! It was wrong. It was a sin. He stayed away, praying desperately that God would take away this longing for the forbidden. And when Michael had died, driving *his* car, Jordan knew it was his fault because he'd hidden that love inside and nurtured it. He had no choice but to disappear from her life. He couldn't hang around Oakburn, knowing that he was in love with his brother's wife. That would have been traitorous.

But what about now?

He still loved her. Jordan had no doubts about that. It was a different kind of love, though. A more mature love. He was prepared to bide his time, let her get used to having him around again. Then he'd test the waters. Maybe in time, please God, she'd see him as something more than the bossy older brother.

"Jordan? Don't you agree?" Caitlin's earnest face frowned up at him. "About waiting," she prompted.

"There's nothing wrong with waiting," Clay insisted. "God will let me know when it's the right time."

"I think He already has." Caitlin's voice was firm. "After ten years Maryann is back, she's single and she has a little girl who needs a father. What more do you need? A lightning bolt?"

Jordan grinned at her vehemence. Caitlin never prevaricated. If there was a decision to be made, she considered both sides, weighed the arguments and chose. If it was a wrong choice, so be it. She dealt with the flak. But she didn't spend time dithering about which route to take. Maybe it was time to take a leaf out of her book.

"She's right, Clay. A man needs to be strong. Forceful. To go after what he wants. If your motives are pure, God will direct you."

Ha! Were his own motives pure? Jordan ignored that nasty little voice and weighed his options.

I love Caitlin he said to himself. *I want to marry her, to help her raise the baby. I want to be able to tell the world that I love her. I don't want to feel ashamed or embarrassed about my feelings any more.*

Yes. That was the truth. So now it was time to lay it all on the line.

Jordan glanced at the other man. Unlike Clay, he was certain he would know the right place and time to tell her. And he'd just have to keep praying that she would get past her fears of abandonment and realize that he wasn't going anywhere without her.

"Jordan? I've just told Clay we'll help him think of some compliments when he comes tomorrow night. Is that okay with you?"

Jordan nodded yes while inside his mind screamed no! If Clay was going to hang around all the time, how would he ever get an opportunity to talk to Caitlin privately?

The following weekend Caitlin allowed herself to sink a little deeper into the softness of her chair as the conversation around her raged on. It was girls' afternoon at Wintergreen, as the Andrews women had officially dubbed it, and it was turning out to be fun.

"Women are more mature. They know what they want and they go after it. Why can't men understand that?" Robyn sighed.

"Because men are romantics." Eliza sipped her tea calmly. "They want us to be helpless, to need them. And we do. But we can also function perfectly well on our own in some matters. That's irritating to someone who sees you as the little woman."

"That's what Jordan's like," Caitlin offered. She flushed a little when Robyn's eyes focused on her. "Well, he is! He thinks I can't vacuum the floor just because I'm pregnant. He insists on bringing in a cleaning service which is silly because I always clean up before they come so they won't think I live in filth.''

A burst of sympathetic laughter agreed.

"It's not funny," she grumbled. "Yesterday I wanted to clean out that hall cupboard. He insisted on bringing this chair out into the hallway and I had to sit there while *he* sorted through the junk left over from the move.'' She shifted uncomfortably. ''I'm pregnant, not paralyzed.''

''Jordan always was pushy. He's the type who walks little old ladies across the street, even when they don't want to go.'' Natasha's voice rang with the certainty of a younger sister from her position on the floor where she reclined against some cushions.

''He's good-hearted though, Nat. You have to give him that. He wouldn't willingly hurt a flea.'' Olivia snatched another brownie and bit into it with a sigh. ''He also eats like a whale and never gains an ounce. Why didn't you pass that gene on to me, Mother?''

''It belonged to your father. And he kept it for the boys. Michael always ate well, too.''

Silence, stark and bare greeted her words. Eliza stared for a moment, then rushed into speech. ''Oh, Caitlin, my dear. I'm so sorry! I didn't mean to upset you.'' She patted her daughter-in-law's hand worriedly. ''Sometimes I forget and, well...'' She stopped.

''It's all right, Eliza. Really. I know Michael's

gone. And I'm sad about it. But I can still talk about him, remember him, without breaking down. I think.''

''Of course you can.'' Natasha's bracing tones were exactly what they all needed. ''Michael might have died, but you didn't. You're alive and it's only natural that you should go on with your life, find someone else to love.'' She studied Caitlin with a frown.

''Is this Clay guy the one you've chosen?''

''Natasha!'' Robyn, Olivia and Eliza all burst out at the same time.

''That's none of your business, Nat. Caitlin doesn't have to explain to you.'' Robyn's rueful glance met Caitlin's. ''Just ignore her.''

''No, of course I won't ignore her.'' Caitlin rubbed a hand over her forehead, wondering where to start.

''Good. So spill it all, Caitlin. I want to know what Clay means to you.'' Natasha's generous mouth curved down. ''I somehow never thought of him as your kind of guy. But what do I know?''

''Exactly what I'd like to know.'' Robyn's eyebrows raised meaningfully, but whatever else she was going to say was drowned by her daughter's cries. ''Come on, sweetie,'' she comforted Eudora. ''Mommy'll kiss it better.''

''Clayton Matthews is just a friend. Someone I'm trying to help out. He's not interested in me at all.'' Would that do it? Caitlin certainly hoped so.

Olivia assumed the lotus position, grinned and popped anther chip into her mouth. ''The only time I ever saw him notice a woman was last week at church. He couldn't take his eyes off Maryann MacGregor.''

"Exactly. He wants to ask her out, but he's a little bit shy.'' Caitlin shifted, knowing that to mention the subject was to elicit unasked-for advice.

"If I remember correctly, his mother had rather a rough time raising all those boys after their father left,'' Eliza murmured, staring out the window at the waning sun. "It's too bad someone didn't take him in hand long ago.''

"So, you're not interested in Clay.'' Natasha took another sip of her soda, lips pursed, eyes narrowed as she shifted fractionally on the sofa. "Who then?''

"Natasha!''

With one accord, the other Andrews women raised their eyebrows and rolled their eyes upward in exasperation. It was a trait they seemed to share with tacit agreement and to Caitlin those eye movements were more expressive than any words they could have uttered.

"Uh, you see, well,'' Caitlin swallowed, searching for the right words. "I'm not really looking for a, um, a man. It's not part of the plan. Not now I mean. That is, I haven't had time to think about it. Not with the baby and everything.''

"You're so young, you don't want to spend your life alone, honey,'' Eliza said. "You need someone to share your life with, someone to laugh with, have fun with, grow old with. Someone you can give your heart to.''

"I don't know anyone like that.''

It was a lie and they knew it as well as she. If she'd learned anything these past weeks it was that Jordan was all of those things. He didn't mind when she was grumpy or angry, or when she lashed out at him. He took it all in stride and, in fact, encouraged her to express herself more often.

Jordan was comfortable, fun, and yet oddly exciting. She got the same rush out of seeing him come through the door that she'd gotten all those years ago when he'd dropped in at Aunt Lucy's to pick her up for youth group.

Was the reason she didn't want to talk about love because thinking about Jordan in that light made her feel guilty? Had she buried her feelings for the older brother when Michael came along, hoping that Michael could make her feel more secure, more in control? Or had she been so hurt by Jordan's obvious insensitivity to her schoolgirl crush, that she'd turned to Michael to pay Jordan back?

Maybe she hadn't been the best wife for Michael. Maybe she'd let herself fall in love with being married instead of being the kind of wife Michael had needed. Had Michael guessed that she'd only gone out with him that first time because she wanted to see Jordan?

Oh, where did all these questions come from? And why now, when it was too late to ask Michael if she'd disappointed him, if he'd known she'd once been in love with his brother? If he'd thought she was using him to get to Jordan?

"Are you planning on going to the fellowship supper next week at church?" Natasha asked.

"Jordan's taking me. He said I needed to get out of the house."

"That's nice." Eliza took Eudora from Robyn and put the little girl on her knee. "You know, Caitlin, I was looking at some old photos last night. Your wedding picture, actually. I know it wasn't that long ago, but you looked so young. You've grown up a lot since then, haven't you?"

"I like to think so." Caitlin closed her eyes to stop the tears that came as she remembered that silly, scared little girl. Had she really changed at all?

"I think you've changed a lot." Olivia looked up from her cross-stitch. "Michael used to say that you were his stabilizer, that you anchored him."

"Not well enough, otherwise he'd never have been driving so wildly." Caitlin felt she had to say it, they were all thinking it anyway.

"Caitlin. That didn't have anything to do with you! You couldn't have stopped him and you know it. Anyway, Michael was God's child. You couldn't have changed God's time no matter what you did." Eliza moved to wrap one arm around Caitlin. "Michael loved you, my dear girl. He thought the sun, moon and stars rolled around your head."

"He would be glad to know you're getting on with your life," Robyn agreed. "Michael loved life too much to want anyone not to live it."

"But I was so stupid. I was so scared that he'd leave me that I hung on too tightly. I'm sure he got tired of that.'' A lump rose in her throat that she couldn't swallow down. ''Maybe I'm bad luck or something, I don't know. But everyone I love seems to leave.''

''Caitlin Andrews you stop that right now!'' Eliza stood up, tall and strong, her voice loving but firm. ''Our God does not deal in luck!

''Yes, you've had a tragic life. But honey, don't let yourself become some kind of a tragic hero. You and Michael loved each other. And God blessed your marriage with Junior here.'' Eliza patted Caitlin's stomach.

''Open your eyes and look around you. God has given you people who care about you. We do.''

The girls' heads nodded in exuberant agreement.

''So does Jordan, and your friends here at Wintergreen. We're your family and we're not going anywhere. So let's get on with life and move into the promised land. Okay?'' Eliza brushed one hand in a tender caress across Caitlin's cheek.

''Okay. I'll try not to dwell in the desert anymore, Eliza.'' Caitlin smiled, grateful that these woman cared enough to stay with her, challenge her.

''And you promise you'll keep your eyes peeled for the wonderful things God is going to do in your life, the wonderful people He sends? You won't shut them out?''

''I promise.''

''Promise what? What's going on here? Good grief! You all look as though you've been peeling onions.'' Jordan, tall, bossy and impossibly dear, stood in the doorway, frowning at all of them.

''Well? Are we going out for dinner or not?''

Caitlin glanced at Robyn, who raised her eyebrows at her sisters, but it was Eliza who finally burst into laughter. They all rose, searching for gloves and coats and purses.

''Yes, son, you're going out for dinner. And Caitlin's going with you. But Robyn and I have to get home. And Olivia's got a date with her hubby. Natasha, now...'' Her voice trailed away. ''I have to think about Natasha,'' they heard her murmur as she tugged on her boots, buttoned her coat and hurried out the door without even saying goodbye. ''There must be someone for her.''

Natasha grimaced, her face sour as she pretended to slug Jordan on the shoulder. ''Thanks a lot, Jordy,'' she grumbled, her face fiery red. ''Now she'll start in on me and heaven knows who she'll drag home! Last month she set up a blind date. A blind date!'' She shook her head dismally. ''He was as mortified as I was.''

''This is my fault?'' Jordan looked completely stumped.

''Yes! You're my big brother. You're supposed to protect me.'' Natasha's forehead suddenly cleared. ''By the way, Caitlin wants to go to Chez Lee. She's simply dying to try their lobster. I told her you wouldn't mind taking her. After all, it is Saturday and you're allowed to stay out late.''

Natasha scurried past to the door, her scarf trailing

behind. "Bye, Caitlin. Don't let him bully you. And make him pay. Big time!"

"What did I do to her?"

"Years of bossiness, Brother dear. Now it's pay-back time." Robyn patted his arm, her eyes glowing with mischief. "But Caitlin really does want lobster. And onion rings. I don't know why. Ask her." She kissed Caitlin, grabbed her bundled-up daughter and headed out the door.

"I've got to go, too," Olivia murmured, tugging on her gloves. She hugged Caitlin close and then fixed her with a stern look. "No desert. Okay?"

Caitlin nodded, smiling as the last sister left.

"No desert? Doesn't she mean dessert? And why not?" Jordan's eyes worked open and closed as he tried to reason out the strange tableau.

"I've got to give you credit, Andrews," Caitlin giggled as she picked up the cups. "You sure know how to clear a room."

"And I wasn't even trying to get them to leave," he marveled. "I wish I knew what I did so I could do it again next time."

Caitlin burst out laughing, happier than she could remember being in months.

He followed her through to the kitchen, his hands full of used napkins and empty chip containers. "So where shall we go for dinner? We haven't got a res-ervation for Chez Lee's so that's out. But otherwise, take your pick."

He lifted the crystal bowl out of her hand and set in on the shelf she'd been stretching to reach. As his hands came down, one brushed the length of her hair, lightly fingering the russet curls, while the other rested on her shoulder.

For a moment, just one small unit of time, Caitlin relaxed against his massaging fingers as they manipulated the taut cord across her shoulder.

"You okay?" His gold eyes searched hers as he eased her into a chair. "No backache?"

"A little." She sat there, her head resting against his side, allowing the tiny thrill of joy to trickle from his fingertips to her heart.

"You're tired. I knew you shouldn't have asked Clay over again last night. It's bizarre, this coaching him in endearments." But his voice was soft and indulgent.

"No, it's not. He really cares for her, Jordan. I can't turn my back on that." She sighed when his fingers moved onto her scalp, easing the bands of pressure that clung there.

"Do you want me to make something? I know you're too tired to go out. I promise I'll sterilize everything when I'm finished. You'll never know I've been here."

Jordan loved cooking almost as much as he hated cleaning up. And yet he was willing to do that for her, too. The small sacrifice brought a smile to her lips.

"I don't think so. But thanks anyway. I'm just not in the mood for anything that's here, in spite of your efforts to bring the entire store home. And we can have lobster another time."

"I'm almost afraid to ask." He sat down in the chair opposite her, his hands gently caressing hers as he spoke. "What are you in the mood for, Caitlin?"

He was so dear, sitting here like this, holding her. Would it be so wrong to love him? To let a tiny piece of her heart thaw enough to pour it out on Michael's brother.

"Caitlin?"

"Hmm?"

"What'll it be?"

"Chicken, I think. Strips. Golden crisp and steaming, with hot mustard sauce to dip them in, and some coleslaw on the side. And lemonade." She closed her eyes, dreaming of it all, and opened them again when she heard his snort of laughter.

"You're kidding, right? Coleslaw? Hot mustard sauce? Lemonade?" His eyes sparkled with laughter, his mouth creased in that teasing grin. "With your stomach? You'll need antacids all night long!"

Caitlin pretended to bristle. "Just because you don't like chicken is no reason I shouldn't enjoy it. I'll call the delivery people." She yanked her hands away from his and stood too quickly, causing the blood to rush to her feet. Caitlin wavered for a moment, then grabbed at the table.

"Are you all right?" His arm came around her shoulders and he helped her walk from the kitchen to the living room, easing her onto the sofa. "There. Put your feet up and watch the television for a while. I'll be back shortly." His eyes glinted with laughter.

"But I'm warning you, the time will come when you won't be able to con me anymore."

Caitlin thrust her nose in the air and sniffed derisively. "As if I'd bother. I'm not helpless, you know," she sputtered, struggling to free herself from the soft cushy comfort of furniture that seemed intent on swallowing her up.

"Close enough." He grinned as she subsided with a sigh, then pressed a kiss to the top of her head and just managed to dodge the pillow she chucked at him. "And don't move or I'll give the chicken to someone else. See you in a bit."

"When I sell this sofa and get something I can get in and out of, you're going to be sorry." She shifted again, then sighed in resignation. "Threats," she called as he walked out of the apartment. "That's what you always use."

"That's because they work," he called back.

As usual Jordan got the last word in.

He was so easy, so much fun, so comfortable to be around. It couldn't be wrong to love a man like that?

Could it?

Chapter Ten

"I take it that waiting a week to get here was worthwhile?" Jordan escorted her out of the posh restaurant, a smile tugging at his mouth. "Chez Lee lived up to your expectations?"

Caitlin smiled as she grasped his helping hand and eased herself into his car. "It was excellent. I don't know when I've enjoyed myself more. Thank you, Jordan."

He didn't answer her until he was inside the car beside her and had eased the vehicle into traffic.

"You're welcome. I'm glad you enjoyed it. I was a little worried about you there for a minute," he joked, his eyes sparkling. "The waiter couldn't do enough. I'm sure he personally inspected every mouthful you ate. But when the maitre d' started hovering, with the dessert tray in his hands, I wondered if we shouldn't ask for some carryout."

Caitlin pursed her lips, considering the idea. "Hey,

you should have suggested it." Then she shook her head. "No, better not. But I find I get that a lot lately. I call it the kid-glove treatment. There's a real advantage to being pregnant, you know."

Jordan nodded his agreement. His mouth opened, then closed, as if he thought better of his reply. Instead, he turned on the CD player and tapped one forefinger against the wheel in tune to a concerto.

It only took a few minutes, then they were pulling up in front of Wintergreen. Caitlin waited for Jordan's assistance. Once out of the car, she wrapped her arm in his as they walked up the driveway.

"You look very pleased with yourself." He opened the door, waited for her to go in, then closed it, watching her curiously.

Caitlin grinned as she unlocked her apartment. She pushed open the door. "I feel wonderful," she enthused. "Spoiled and pampered and utterly coddled."

He grinned. "Wonderful is one of your favorite words tonight, it seems." His golden eyes sparkled with fun. "Well, it was a wonderful evening!"

"Don't hold back Jordan. Forget modesty and humility. Tell me how you really feel," Caitlin teased in return, brushing her knuckles across his lean cheek.

It was meant to be funny, but the tension in the room suddenly increased tenfold when he caught her fingers and pressed them to his mouth.

"All right, I will." The words were soft. In the glow of the single lamp she could see only shadows as they moved across his face. His eyes were dark-gold, molten, burning her in their intensity. He set her boots aside but stayed kneeling there.

"I'm in love with you, Lyn. I have been for a long time. I want to marry you." He lifted his hand up into the light, snapping open the lid of a black velvet box.

Caitlin gasped at the glittering magnificence that sparkled out at her. It was an exquisite diamond, pear-shaped and perched atop a wide gold band. Slowly she tore her eyes from it to the man who knelt in front of her.

"M-marry you?"

"Yes. I want to be able to come home to you every night, to stay here with you, instead of lying at home, alone, wondering if you're all right, if you need me. I want to be here for you and the baby. I want us to live and love and laugh together until the end. I love you, Lyn."

It sounded great, wonderful, inviting. It was the kind of fairy-tale life she had always wanted and never found.

It was too good to be true.

"Jordan, I don't know what to say."

"Yes would be nice." He smiled that silly, crooked smile that tugged at her heartstrings. "Maybe would be almost acceptable." He stopped when the tears began. "Don't Caitlin. Don't cry. Please?"

"I'm sorry. I can't help it. You've been marvelous, Jordan. So good to me when I was so cranky. And I've appreciated it more than you know. I don't know how I would have managed without you and your family here."

"But?" He leaned back on his haunches, hands falling to his side, the ring lying in her lap. "There is a but, isn't there?"

"I can't marry you, Jordan." Dear Lord it hurt to say that, to see the flash of anguish cross his eyes.

"Why?"

She heard the anger in that single word and hated herself for causing him pain.

"It wouldn't be right."

"Are you nuts?" He grinned, throwing his arms wide. "It would be fantastic. I love you. I want to marry you. I want us to live together as husband and wife."

"I'm Michael's wife." The words came out cold and harsh, bursting his exuberant bubble.

His eyes narrowed, lips stretched tight and thin.

"Were! You *were* Michael's wife. He's gone, Lyn. But I'm here, alive. And I'm still in love with you."

"Still?" What was he saying? Caitlin didn't know where to look or what to say. She hated to cause the hurt in his eyes and yet she simply couldn't marry him. Not with fear clinging to her like yesterday's news.

"I've loved you for years." His hands closed around her face, his palms firm against her cheeks as he forced her to look at him. "I loved you in high school, Caitlin."

"But you..." She avoided the yearning she saw hidden behind the playful banter and teasing familiarity. She couldn't let herself feel that.

"Look at me, Caitlin." His hands tenderly forced

her chin up, coaxing her to see what she wanted to have and didn't dare take.

"I loved you. But I was boring, wrapped up in my computers. I wasn't the kind of boyfriend you needed. Michael was young and vibrant. You needed someone like him, someone who wasn't dull and staid and too old for you. Someone who would help you to branch out, live a little."

"That's why you dumped me? To give Michael a chance?"

He nodded. "Yes. But also to give you a chance. I was older than you, Lyn. Sure you were brainy and two years ahead of your peers, but you needed that two years to mature. I wanted you to have that time, to sample life, go out with kids who'd have your interests." He grimaced. "Computer nerds aren't much fun."

She heard it all. Every word sank into her brain. But she couldn't believe she hadn't figured it out. Caitlin picked up the ring case and turned it round and round, then set it on the coffee table.

"And you didn't think you owed it to me to tell me?" Indignation reared its head. "You didn't think I had enough brains and common sense to tell you whom I preferred?"

"It was pretty obvious, wasn't it?" Jordan's damning words cut her protests short. "You started going out with him two days after I told you I couldn't see you anymore."

"Do you know why?" Caitlin resisted the temptation to touch him.

"I went out with Michael so I could see you. That's why. I thought seeing you like that was better than nothing. So yes, I went out with him, I went to the football games with him, I came over for dinner as often as I could. I let myself be included in your family because I couldn't pull away."

For once in his life Jordan Andrews appeared to have nothing to say.

"Eventually you went away to college and Michael and I were chumming around more and more. When we graduated, we chose the same college, took some of the same classes. We even rode home together at vacation."

"And eventually you fell in love. Right?" Hurt shimmered in Jordan's golden gaze. His hands clenched in his lap, belying the smile on his face. "I knew it would happen."

"It didn't happen right away. It sort of grew on us. Michael was all the things I wasn't and, I admit, I liked that. He wasn't afraid of anything. Life was like a big game to him and he was determined not to miss a thing."

She fell into a reverie, thinking about the many heated disagreements they'd had over his carefree attitude. How many times had she chided him for skipping an afternoon of work in order to fly a kite in the park or drive to the beach for a swim? How many times had he coaxed her away from her post-grad studies to go to a party or plan tennis or anything else that took his fancy?

"Caitlin, Michael is gone."

"Do you think I don't know that?" Caitlin slowly got up, stepped past him and walked to the window, staring out at the cold, black night. "It was my fault he died. Mine."

"It wasn't! He drove too fast under conditions that were not suitable. He took my car and even I know it was an accident." He stood behind her, not touching her.

As she stood there, Caitlin could feel the heat from his body, the sizzle that flickered between their minds every time Jordan came into the room. It had been the same back then.

"The night before he died we had an argument. Michael was angry at me, very angry. He said I was trying to hide from life."

She drew in a deep breath and turned to face Jordan.

"Michael asked me if I'd married him so I could live vicariously through him. He asked me if I didn't think I'd have been better off with you. Safer."

She could hear him suck in his breath and winced at the suffering she'd caused. But she couldn't stop now. She wouldn't.

"I told him I loved him. I told him I only wanted to be married to him. To be his wife. I promised I'd never be a drag on him again. I was so scared he'd leave, I would have promised him anything. Anyway, he said he forgave me. The next day he borrowed your car. The police say he was driving too fast for conditions."

"And you think that he took some extra risks just

to prove that he could handle things?" Jordan shook
his head. "It isn't true, Lyn. Michael had been driving
that way for years. Dad used to lecture him on it, but
Michael always laughed it off—said he knew what he
was doing."

Caitlin shivered as the icy cold draft from the window washed over her. She'd have to get new storm
windows, she decided absently.

"That doesn't matter. The point is, if he hadn't felt
he had to prove that he could take risks and survive,
I don't think he would have gone. My husband may
have gone to his death believing I never loved him.
That's what nags at me." She swallowed down her
tears and turned to face him. "There could never be
anything between us, Jordan. It would be like betray-
ing Michael's trust in me. I told him I loved him."

She wondered about that now, wondered if she'd
really loved him the way she should have.

"Lyn, you were always faithful to Michael. You
loved him the best you knew. You were his wife. You
didn't betray him by urging caution."

"How can you be so sure?" Caitlin jerked her head
up to glare at him. "How can you know that? I
don't."

"But—"

"Every day I ask myself if I supported him the way
he needed. Did I tell him that I loved him when I
should have? Did he *believe* that I only wanted him,
that there wasn't anybody else for me by then? Was
I telling the truth?" She shook her head.

"I can't be sure, Jordan. I can't be sure. And I can't

help wondering if that's why God took him, because I didn't measure up."

There, it was said. The whole terrible awful truth. Let Jordan see how ugly her soul really was.

She wasn't surprised when Jordan didn't say anything.

"I thank you for your kindness and your friendship, Jordan. And I appreciate your help more than I can say. But friendship is all I can ever share with you."

"Like friendship is all you share with Clay and Garrett and all the others?"

She heard the frustration in his voice and felt bad for it. But there was nothing she could do about it. There was no way he could ever make her believe that Michael's death hadn't been a punishment for her failures as a wife.

"Clay and Gar are friends. And, thanks to you, I'm learning that I need friends in my life. But the past, the things that have happened to me, have made me who I am. I can't ignore them, Jordan."

She knew he wanted to say something, that he was about to tell her off. But his pager beeped and would not be ignored. Minutes later, as if through a fog, Caitlin heard him agree to fly to Minneapolis."

"Caitlin?"

She faced him.

"I have to go. A very important client has just lost his entire system to a virus. I've got to see what I can do to help."

"Of course." She forced a smile. "Go. Save the hard drive or whatever it is."

"I will." He nodded. "But first I need to say something. Will you come and sit down?"

She allowed him to press her into a chair and stayed there when he squatted in front of her. She even met his gaze when his hands closed around her and little jolts of electricity shot up her arm.

"Listen to me, Lyn. I haven't got much time."

"I'm listening."

"I loved my brother. So did you. You were his wife and you did everything right. I know it, and I think deep down, you do too. Michael knew you loved him. I don't believe he ever doubted it. Nor should you. You were the best possible wife a man could ask for."

She smiled blankly. They were just words. He had to say them. What else could he say?

"But that was the past. I'm here now, Caitlin. Me. Jordan. And I love you here and now. There is nothing you could tell me, nothing you could say, that would change that love. And whether you believe in it or not doesn't change the fact that I love you. I always will."

He grinned that irrepressible grin. One hand pushed a swath of hair back off her forehead. With his forefinger he traced the lines of her eyebrows, her nose, the curve of her mouth and the stubborn tilt of her chin.

"You see, sweetheart, it's kind of like God's love for us. Whether we see Him or not, believe in Him or not, trust in Him or not, His love stays. Permanently. And there is nothing we can do to change that.''

He stood then, sighed and moved away. One hand snagged his jacket and he flung it on. "It doesn't matter how long it takes you to trust in me. It doesn't matter when you call or what you ask of me, I'll always be there for you. Always. After all this time, my love isn't going to go away. It's going to grow and grow and grow. And whenever you're ready, I'll be waiting. Okay?''

When he didn't move or look away she finally nodded.

''There's just one more thing, Lyn. Though I'd like to, I can't be here all the time. So if you need help or assurance or just someone to calm the fear, you pray and ask God for help. He'll be there. And He'll answer. You just have to ask.''

"Goodbye, Jordan." Tears formed at the ends of her lashes, big, fat tears that she couldn't control. "Thank you for everything you've done. Be safe.''

"It's not goodbye. I'll be back, Lyn. You'll see. But meanwhile, I'm leaving you in God's hands. You couldn't be safer.''

Then he pulled her into his arms and pressed his lips on hers, kissing her with the purpose and intensity of a man who knows exactly what he wants and has no doubt he'll attain it.

"Goodbye, little mama. I love you.''

"I love you, too, Jordan." But there was no one to hear the whispered words. No one but the wind as it whistled in through the open door.

Chapter Eleven

"The weather office is warning everyone to stay off the roads this Tuesday afternoon as sleet and rain combine with snow and high winds to create a huge outdoor skating rink. The storm is expected to continue until well into tomorrow."

Great, Caitlin thought, as she shut off the television. She was stuck at home without a single soul for company.

"It's the perfect time for a little one-on-one with the kitchen," she decided and pulled on a pair of rubber gloves. Two minutes later she was tugging one off to answer the phone.

"I'm fine, Eliza. No, I haven't been out. Beth is at the store and she intends to stay there overnight just in case the flower coolers go out. Maryann and her daughter are visiting out of town."

She paused and listened.

"Really it's fine. I've lots of food, plenty of wood

for the fire, and several really good books. I'll be snuggled in for the duration.''

By the time she rang off, Eliza seemed satisfied that Caitlin was only a phone call away.

''At least now she won't get in her car and drive over here,'' Caitlin muttered, rubbing a sore spot in the center of her back. Two minutes later she heaved herself up from scrubbing the baseboards to answer the phone again.

''Yes, Robyn, your mother just called. Everything's fine. No, I'm not doing anything too strenuous,'' she lied. ''Yes, I'll be fine.''

''Well, whatever you do, just sit tight and relax,'' her sister-in-law ordered before she rang off.

''I'd love to relax,'' Caitlin muttered wryly. ''But the phone keeps ringing.''

With a determined nudge, the worry of being alone receded to the back of her mind. Once the kitchen was clean, she concentrated on removing the mildew from the grout in the bathroom.

By six o'clock there was a glassy sheet of crystal-clear ice in front of the house and down the street as far as she could see. Freezing cold rain dashed down to the ground, sticking to whatever substance it met. Caitlin cringed when she spied the power lines, sagging with their ice-encrusted load.

''It can't be that bad,'' she told herself sternly. ''Mr. Wilson just drove into his yard.''

Unfortunately Mr. Wilson couldn't stop and Caitlin winced as his car plowed into the perfect splendor of his beautiful new oak-paneled garage door.

"That's going to cost some money," she murmured, watching as the elderly man carefully worked his way past the car and up the walk, slipping and sliding from side to side. "But at least he wasn't hurt."

She heaved a sigh of relief when he finally made it inside.

The telephone interrupted her musings and Caitlin absently rubbed her stomach as she answered. These Braxton-Hicks were getting really fierce.

"It's me, honey. Stan says this is our last chance to make it over. Are you sure you don't want us to come?"

"Of course not, Eliza. It's awful outside. Besides, I'm perfectly fine and I can do whatever needs doing around here without you guys risking your lives on those roads."

"You're sure? No baby yet?"

"Of course I'm sure and that question is getting old very quick." She paused, stuffing down frustration. "I'm just going to have some dinner, watch a little television and then head for bed. What could be simpler?"

"And you're not having any contractions? Your water hasn't broken?" Eliza's worried voice carried clearly over the line. "You're past your date, Caitlin, so you have to monitor these things very carefully now."

"I know. And I have been. But there's nothing unusual here, Eliza. Junior is just pushing a little. He thinks his momma is a football, I guess.'' She drew circles on her stomach, hoping to quiet the agile baby.

''Huh! Sounds like Jordan! He was determined not to leave without doing some damage. That boy can't be swayed once he makes up his mind.''

''No, I guess not. Any word from him?'' She hated asking it, but Jordan hadn't phoned her once in the past three days. She missed him, the sound of his booming voice, his capable hands, his tender glances.

''Not a word, though he often doesn't call when he's away on a job. He just shows up once the work is done. I hope he's not flying tonight!''

Something else to worry about, Caitlin thought after hanging up the phone. Imagining Jordan in an airplane in this ice storm made her physically sick and as the bile rose she rushed into the bathroom.

''Why is it that nothing with this pregnancy is going according to the books?'' she asked herself later, having recovered enough strength to down a few more tablespoons of the lukewarm broth. ''Evening sickness in the ninth month is not nice!''

She gasped and grabbed her stomach as a fierce cramp seized her belly.

''Now you don't like tomato soup?'' she gasped, breathing more deeply as the sensation eased, then passed. ''What a fussy kid.''

Caitlin stood carefully, rubbing her back as she inched forward toward the sofa. If she could just make it there and lie down, everything would be fine.

''Leaving the kitchen,'' she announced and then gasped as warm wet fluid gushed down her legs. ''Oh, no! My water broke!'' She hobbled through to the laundry room, found some clean clothes and changed as quickly as she could. She was just easing on her slippers when the lights flickered.

''No,'' she cried out, gripping the closet door. ''Please not that!''

The lights stayed on until she arrived in the living room. Then, suddenly, everything was dark. A crack outside coincided with a flesh-searing contraction that threatened to tear her insides out.

''Oh, God!'' she breathed with heartfelt appeal. ''The baby's coming and I'm all alone.''

The Lamaze lessons that seemed so simple mere weeks ago fled her mind and it was all Caitlin could do to sink into her chair and puff her way through one contraction after another, wondering at the strength and intensity of them.

Outside something shattered, then thundered to the ground, reminding her of the past. It had been exactly like this the night her parents had died. Her father had been outside fixing a shutter when the call came about her grandmother.

They'd scrambled into the car and started out for the hospital, careening from left to right over the slick surface, missing cars, posts and red lights by inches. Only they hadn't missed the last one. A semi-truck, unable to stop on the glare ice, plowed into them with a sickening crunch Caitlin could still hear today.

How long had she lain there in the car, waiting for whatever took her parents to kill her, too? How may times had she begged God to send someone to help her mother, to stop that awful wheezing sound she made with every breath?

She came back to reality with a thud. How long had she been lying here, panting her way through one pain after the other?

Oh, God, please send me some help. Why didn't I let Eliza come over? Why was I too proud to ask for help?

The questions boiled through her mind in lucid moments when she wasn't concentrating on her abdomen. During a particularly long lull Caitlin managed to light the big eucalyptus candle that sat on her coffee table, but the light was faint and flickering in the huge room. No streetlights shone outside.

Please God, send me someone. I'm sorry I haven't trusted You. I know I was wrong. I just couldn't shake off the past. But I never really stopped believing in You. Not really. Please forgive me?

The next contraction was the most painful yet and she whimpered in agony, wondering how she would get out of this fix. The telephone! She reached for it, dialed 911 and found the line dead.

Caitlin wanted to light the fire to ward off some of the chill that was seeping through her thin blouse, but she couldn't seem to make it to the fireplace before yet another contraction hit. She breathed it through, reminding herself of the two techniques she could recall. Breathe deeply and relax.

The minutes dragged past, counted off by the mantel clock. Caitlin lost track of everything but the fact that she and the baby were in trouble.

Call upon Me and I will hear you in the day of trouble.

The old Sunday school verse her father had recited so often popped into her mind.

"Okay, God. I'm calling. Please help me in this awful time of trouble. I'm afraid for the baby. Please don't take him. Please God."

She huffed and puffed her way through another pain and then froze as a noise at the front door caught her attention.

Burglars! Looting homes and shops while there was no one to catch them. What would happen when they saw the place wasn't empty?

Caitlin prayed harder, breathed deeper, and counted longer as the contractions dragged out. She strained to hear what was going on at the front door, but her attention strayed, her mind revisiting the terrifying looting scenes she'd seen on television just last week.

I'm here. I've always been here. Call on Me.

"Please, God," she whispered, shrinking as far back into the chair as she could. "Please help me. Send me someone. Please."

The front door creaked open and a shadow inched its way froward. Caitlin could see it all from her chair. Belatedly she wished she'd closed her apartment door. But she'd wanted to waylay anyone who could help her.

The person headed into her living room, carefully edging around the furniture with tentative groping hands. He was big, far too big for her to overpower. As he came closer, Caitlin prayed harder and refused to give in to the agony that racked her body. She bit her lip, closed her eyes and counted to twenty.

"Ouch!" A thud, a crash, and then a voice that was loud and unmistakable. "Good grief!"

"Jordan?" Caitlin could have wept with relief when his face, finally lit by that one flickering candle, swam into her tear-filled view.

He lit the three candles clenched in his hand and stood them on the table, eyes narrowing as he studied her. "Are you all right? I've been phoning for ages, but the line isn't working. Mom said she'd talked to you earlier, but I thought I'd check anyway."

Caitlin couldn't answer, she couldn't move. The best she could manage were short shallow puffs that kept the oxygen moving through her body.

"Caitlin? What's wrong?" He was there, beside her, holding her hands as she let the crest of it roll over her.

"I have to go to the hospital, Jordan. Now. Ooh, here comes another one!" She held on to his hand like a lifeline, refusing to let go until sanity returned.

"You chose tonight to go into labor? Honestly, Caitlin!" A ghost of a grin spread across his pale face. "You are the most stubborn woman I have ever known. I suppose you thought you'd do this alone, too!"

He stopped, winced, flexed his fingers and then held them out again. "Come on, kiddo. Hang on to me. Just keep breathing."

Caitlin renewed her grip on him and prepared for the next wave of unwavering pain. "As if I could stop breathing. I'm beginning to wonder if Robyn was right about you.'' She closed her eyes, concentrated on the searing agony going on inside her body and puffed her way through the contraction.

"Don't you start with me,'' she heard him mutter in a warning that belied his tender touch as he lifted her up and carried her slowly but surely to the front door.

"It's the lousiest night of the year to be driving, you know.'' Jordan's voice was quiet, conversational, with just a hint of steel running through it. "There are lines down everywhere because of the ice. For a woman who doesn't like to live dangerously you sure chose a funny time to have this baby.''

"He chose it. Not me. Ow!''

"But we'll make it, Lyn. We'll make it just fine. You keep hanging on to me.''

"As if,'' she puffed, tightening her hand on his shoulder, "I could do...*puff, puff*...anything else.''

He set her carefully inside his car, did up the seat belt and raced around to climb in the other side. She saw him fumble in his jacket for a moment before his cell phone appeared.

Another contraction hit and Caitlin heard little except Jordan's fierce order to have a doctor standing by.

"Jordan?''

"Yes, sweetheart?'' He revved the engine and slowly backed out of her drive. "What is it?''

"I'm scared, Jordan. Really scared. The contractions came awfully fast after my water broke.'' She swallowed and looked him straight in the eye. "Do you think my baby is all right?"

"I think your baby is just fine, darlin'. A little pushy, maybe, but hey, I'm in favor of pushiness." He grinned, his eyes glittering. "Still, we've got to get you to the hospital now. Couldn't hurt to get a second opinion. Will you trust me to do that?"

Trust him? Of course she trusted him. Jordan was a man of his word. But what if the streets were too icy? What if they had an accident? What if they couldn't get through? The worries swirled around her, sucking her in like an eddy of current.

"Lyn? Sweetheart, if you were thinking about letting God back inside, now would be a really good time. If you trust in Him, ask Him to help us, I know He won't let us down. Can you do that?"

Caitlin stiffened, preparing herself for whatever lay ahead. And then something tweaked at her brain.

"I did pray," she mumbled. "I prayed that God would send someone and He sent you." The very thought of it held her speechless for long tense moments. It was amazing! It was wonderful. It was... God. Talking to her!

He'd answered. She'd called and He'd answered her prayer.

"Just keep praying, honey. Your track record can only get better." Jordan patted her hand, shifted gears and started slowly down the glassy street, steering first left, then right to avoid the downed power lines that littered the area. "Trust God, Lyn. He won't disappoint you."

But Caitlin heard him only vaguely. For some reason the contractions had slowed. Her eyes took in the ravaged streets, the cars that slipped and slid across the road into other cars, smashing metal and grinding bumper to bumper. As Jordan fishtailed his car out of a skid, she was back to the night her parents had died.

"Ice storms are killers," she whispered, mesmerized by the flicker of sparks that shot out from a live wire just fifty feet ahead.

Jordan spared her one quick glance before he jerked the wheel to the right to turn down a different street. "You let God worry about the storm. You just keep praying."

"Watch out," she said as a car in front of them spun on a slick spot.

"It's all right, Caitlin. We're fine. God will take care of us."

"He didn't take care of me. Not at all." She peered out through the windshield, nodding as streetlight after streetlight flickered, then died.

"When my mother was in the car, dying, she told me, 'Be a good girl, Caitlin. Be strong.'" She nodded. "I'll be strong. I will be. I have to be."

Jordan fought to grasp the thread of what she was saying. She'd been in the car with her parents when they'd died? Why hadn't anyone ever told him? Caitlin had heard her mother take her last breath. She'd listened to the last bit of advice her mother had to give.

Be strong.

It was an awful lot to ask of a ten-year-old child.

And yet Caitlin had been strong, far stronger than anyone should have to be. Bit by bit understanding flowed into his brain.

This was why she was so determined to go through life alone. It was what she'd always done when life threw a curveball. Be strong. He smiled grimly. Caitlin Andrews was the strongest woman he'd ever met. But it was time for her to learn to lean on someone else.

"Caitlin? Listen sweetheart, we're almost there. The hospital's right ahead. Can you hear me, darling?"

"Hurts," she whispered. "Hurts bad."

"I know, darlin'." He swallowed, carefully edging past the cars and trucks that lined the hospital entrance. He'd have to go around.

"If we trust God, He will always come through for us. Your mom and dad trusted God to take care of you and here you are, getting ready to be a mommy. Just trust a little bit more now. Just a little more. God will take care of you."

"Hard to trust, Jordan. So hard. Hurts to love." She sounded weak, her breathing short, gasping.

Jordan's heart thundered in his chest, but he refused to give up. His brain kept up a steady petition to heaven as he negotiated around the various vehicles that littered the area.

He parked in front of the emergency door. "Here we are, Lyn."

"Don't leave me," she whimpered as he stepped outside of the car.

Jordan hurried around to the other side, opened the door and lifted her into his arms. "I'm not going anywhere, Lyn. I'll be right here beside you all the way."

"Ooh! Here we go again," she groaned, her fingers twisting in his hair as she wrapped one arm around his neck.

Jordan wanted to groan himself. He wondered if he'd be bald at the end of all this. When her other fist twisted up a handful of his shirt, Jordan lengthened his stride. He had to get her inside, and fast. Thank goodness for the portico that sheltered the driveway from the ice.

He set her down in a wheelchair and gave the doctors the pertinent information, watching as they wheeled her off into a labor room.

"I'll be right there, Lyn," he called to her. "As soon as you get into that bed properly. Just keep trusting."

She blinked, peering up at him as the door closed shut between them. Jordan winced at the sad hurt look in her eyes. She needed her faith now more than ever.

"Please help her," he whispered as he waited for her to reappear. "Please renew her faith and trust and help her to believe. She needs You now more than ever."

He opened his eyes when someone's hand pressed his arm. A nurse, stern but with kindly eyes stood peering up at him.

"She's in hard labor, son. And she's going to need someone to keep her spirits up. It won't be easy, so if you can't do it, you'd better say so right now."

"I can do it," he told her. "I can do whatever needs to be done. There's no way you're getting rid of me now." He visually dared her to try.

To his surprise she smiled.

"Good," she nodded. "Then hang on for the ride."

Chapter Twelve

"**I**f you even think of uttering one more chicken joke, I'm going to rearrange that handsome face. Ooh!" Caitlin's meager grin twisted into a grimace as she braced herself, hands closing around Jordan's arm.

"Breathe," he told her. "In and out, just let it go. That's good, darlin'. Very good." He kept murmuring compliments until she finally relaxed, her face drained and white.

"I am breathing, you know," Caitlin complained, her fingers unwrapping from his forearm. "It's not as if I can just stop!"

Jordan wondered if he'd have any skin left there when this baby finally arrived.

"Okay, sweetheart. Okay. You're doing fine. Everything's fine." He repeated the phrase as much to reassure himself as her.

"Stop telling me the same thing over and over."

She didn't look like she was joking. "I know what's fine and this isn't it!"

"All right." He kept his voice amiable. "What would you like me to say instead?"

"Caitlin Andrews is the smartest woman I know," she gasped, and returned her fingers to the permanent indentations in his arm. "Here we go again!"

"Caitlin Andrews is the smartest, most beautiful, least stubborn, most caring, forgiving and absolutely amazing woman I know," he whispered, brushing her hair back and dabbing at her forehead with a washcloth. He pressed a kiss there for good measure.

"That's more like it," she grunted.

Jordan could see her tiring little by little with each contraction. It had been hours and nothing seemed to be happening.

"Okay, darlin'. I'm here. Hang on. Here we go again." He brushed his hand over her tummy in circles, just the way the nurse had told him to. "Okay, Lyn. That's right. You're doing great! Junior's coming right along."

"He's sure taking his time." She puffed, face taut with tiredness. "Can I have an ice chip?"

"You've already had…"

"Andrews, give me that ice!"

She definitely wasn't joking now. Jordan slipped the chip between her teeth and watched as she sucked at it greedily.

"I'm just going to check you again, Caitlin. Try not to tense up." Dr. Warren smiled, her eyes sparkling above her mask. "You've certainly got a good helper in this guy. He doesn't complain at all."

"He's not allowed to," Caitlin muttered, her eyes dull. "He insisted on being here, and I'm not letting him go home early."

"That's for sure." Jordan grinned to show he didn't hold any grudges. "She likes to drag things out."

He kept his focus on Caitlin, but didn't miss the doctor's narrowed eyes, or quick flash of concern. When she raised her eyebrows, he nodded.

"Caitlin, Jordan's just about worn-out. I want him to go sit down and get a cup of coffee. Is that okay?"

Caitlin frowned, glancing from one to the other.

"You're leaving?"

"No way. Just getting a drink. You're not very good about sharing your ice." Jordan grinned, patted her hand and leaned down to brush her cheek with his lips. "I'll be right back, I promise. Meanwhile, the nurse will stay with you."

He gave her a thumbs up and headed for the door. "What's wrong?" he asked the doctor the moment they cleared the doorway. "What's the matter?"

Dr. Warren sighed. "She's not progressing at all and I'm getting concerned. Dilation hasn't changed. According to the monitor, the baby's heart isn't recovering as fast as we'd like after the contractions, either. It's probably tiring. So is Caitlin. I don't like it."

"What's the answer?"

"C-section. Get the baby out and give the mom a

break.'' Dr. Warren's eyes met his. ''You don't think she'll go for it.''

''I doubt it. Caitlin likes to be in control. She can't believe that things will be okay if she trusts someone else. I can't imagine she'll agree to an operation. Can we wait a bit?''

Dr. Warren shook her head, her forehead pleated in a frown.

''Not much longer. I think we should start preparing her for it. I don't see any other way.''

''I'll try to talk her into it, but you might just have to go ahead and operate.''

Jordan turned to go back in, his mind busy. Before he entered the room, he pulled out his cell phone and dialed his parents' home number to update them on Caitlin's condition. And once more he pleaded with them not to risk driving to the hospital.

''You're getting tired, Lyn. Try to relax.'' He said as he entered the room, though he knew it was a stupid thing to say as soon as the words came out. Evidently she agreed.

''Gee thanks, Jordan. Okay, I'll just close my eyes and pretend it's not happening. Ow!'' Her fingers dug into his arm extra deep. ''Sorry. Your method doesn't work very well. Oh, I want to go home.''

He stared at the fetal monitor, willing it to speed up. A moment later her eyes opened and her gaze followed his.

''It's taking longer for it to go up, isn't it?'' she whispered, her face growing even paler. ''I thought it was my imagination.''

"The doctors are getting a bit concerned," he told her plainly. "They're thinking about a cesarean."

"No way!" She puffed her way through the next pain, pinching his arm and glaring at him all the while. "I'm not letting myself be put under so I'll be helpless to fight for this child. No way! Besides, an operation would be hard on him, too."

"Lyn, remember what I said about trusting. God will take care of things if we trust in Him."

"It's so hard. Ooh." Finally she got through the crest of it and then watched the monitor as closely as everyone else.

"I'm afraid there's not a lot of choice, Caitlin. That baby needs to come out. Now. We're going to take every precaution." Dr. Warren looked stern. "We can't afford much more time."

Her face blanched, her big green eyes full of fear. "I'm scared, Jordan. It'll be like in the car, black and lonely, all by myself. I can't do that again. What if they make a mistake?"

"No one's going to make a mistake tonight, Caitlin. Dr. Warren is the smartest baby doctor I know."

Also the only one, but Jordan wasn't going into that now.

"And besides, God's in control. Isn't He, Lyn?" Maybe if he got her to admit it, she'd relax.

"I don't know." She hesitated, staring up at him, never looking away as the contraction tore through her body, her voice a faint whimper of agony.

Jordan stared at her intently, allowing some of her

fear to penetrate his brain. It was time to deal with this cleanly. Here and now.

"I want everyone to leave. Just for a moment." Dr. Warren tipped her head to one side and he nodded. "Just for a minute."

When they were gone, Jordan bent over Caitlin. He brushed his hand over her forehead tenderly, willing her to feel his love.

"Caitlin, I know you've had it rough. It's been a long hard path and it's taken a lot out of you. But you have to let the doctor help you. Help the baby. You have to face the fear, let someone else take control now. You can't do it all alone anymore."

"But what if something goes wrong?"

"There's always that possibility, sweetheart. But life is full of chances. You have to trust that God will do what's right for both of you. You have to get rid of the fear now. This is no place for being frightened. This is the place to put your trust in One who knows and cares about you."

"But to go under that anesthetic, to miss out on everything? Besides, anesthetics can slow down the baby's heart rate."

"I care, Lyn. And I'm not going anywhere. I love you and I love the baby. I'll be here. I'll be Michael's proxy, just for a while. I'll be here to welcome this baby into the world. I'll make sure everything's okay."

"And if something happens to me, you'll take over? You'll look after my baby?" Her lips trembled as she uttered the unthinkable.

Jordan placed his fingers across them, stopping the words. "Nothing is going to happen while God is in control. And He is, isn't He, Lyn?"

She nodded slowly, finally admitting it. Jordan heaved a sigh of relief.

"That's right. And this baby is His special gift to you."

"That's why I don't want anything to happen." She looked lost and forlorn in the big, sterile room with its chrome machines glittering nearby.

"That's why you've got to rely on God, to trust in Him. He's bigger, more powerful than the doctors. He'll take care of you both, if you'll ask Him."

He prayed fervently as the silence stretched between them. He could see her wrestling with the issue, trying to resolve it as she strained through another contraction. Finally she nodded.

"All right. I'll ask Him." She closed her eyes and prayed, voice soundless but lips moving.

He waited, willing the fetal monitor to speed up and desperately praying when it didn't. Lyn watched too, chewing her lip until the heartbeat finally resumed, her breath whooshing out in a sigh of relief.

"Okay, I'll let them operate."

"God *is* going to get you through this, Lyn," he murmured. His hand held hers firmly as the nurse injected a solution into the drip bag.

She whispered just before she lost consciousness, "I trust Him."

Jordan couldn't help a wash of relief as he watched the nurses readying her for surgery.

"Okay, let's move. We've got a baby to deliver, people." Dr. Warren patted Jordan's hand, holding him back as the nurses rolled Caitlin out of the room and down the hall. "She'll be fine."

"I promised I'd be there for the baby." He met her frown head on. "I intend to keep that promise."

After a long pause, the doctor nodded. "Very well. I'll let you watch. Under one condition. You don't faint on me. I haven't got time for a fainter. I've got enough to deal with."

"I won't faint," he told her, following her down the hall to the OR. "There's too much at stake."

The nurse swathed him in baggy green clothes and then showed him where to stand.

He held Caitlin's hand as the surgical team moved in. "I'm not going anywhere, Lyn. I'm right here."

"She's ready?" Dr. Warren waited for the anesthetist's nod. "Okay, folks. Let's get that baby here. Now."

Jordan didn't hear anything else. He focused his prayers on heaven, pouring an unremitting barrage upward as he watched the face he loved more than life.

"Please help her now. Please. She needs this baby to affirm Your love. Keep them both in the shelter of Your arms."

He didn't know how long he prayed. He only became aware of the others in the room when the nurse touched his arm. He let go of Caitlin's hand and set it gently back on the bed, reassured by the steady rise and fall of her chest.

"Here she is," the nurse chirped, her countenance glorious. "A gorgeous baby girl." She settled the tiny bundle in his arms, her hands at the ready in case he failed this first test.

Jordan gulped.

A girl, a tiny perfect little girl.

Michael's daughter.

She had a patch of reddish brown hair and clear pink skin that felt delicately thin and oh, so soft when he grazed a hand over her flailing arm.

"Hello, baby," he whispered, smiling as her tiny fingers closed around his thumb. "Welcome to our world."

Time stood still as the baby lay in his arms. His brother's child. Alive and healthy. Jordan whispered a thank-you to heaven at the blessed weight of her in his arms. She opened her eyes, huge blue eyes that reminded him of his brother, and blinked up at him. He thought he could see a question there.

"Your daddy couldn't be here and your mommy's sleeping," he whispered. "You gave her quite a time. Anyway, I'm here to make sure nothing bad happens. I'll always be here. Whenever you need me." He wasn't aware of the passage of time or the other voices in the room. All he could see was the blind trust in those precious eyes.

A flash of light obscured his vision for a moment. Then the nurse held out a picture.

"She'll want to know you were there to greet her baby." Her voice was soft and caring.

"Thank you," Jordan managed to whisper. When

she held out her arms for the baby, he fought the urge to keep her nestled close to his heart. "Is she all right?"

"She's perfect. Wouldn't you say so, Dr. Warren?"

The doctor was stripping off her gloves. She stood for a moment, watching as Caitlin was wheeled into recovery. Then her glance came back to the baby, now curled up in an isolette.

"She's doing very well. Her color is good, her Apgar rating was high. I'm not anticipating any problems." She laid a hand on his arm. "Caitlin is fine, too. Everything went very smoothly."

"I'll go sit with her until she wakes up."

Dr. Warren followed him out. "She's going to be upset."

"I know." He didn't want to think about just how furiously angry Caitlin would be. "But you tell me, was there another choice?"

The doctor shook her head, her eyes serious. "Not in my opinion."

"Then I can live with whatever comes. They're both alive and that's what I prayed for."

She led him toward the recovery room, let him wait outside until Caitlin was ready. Then when the small russet-haired form was wheeled back to her room, Jordan sank down wearily on a stool beside the bed and took Caitlin's small, delicate hand once more, tracing the veins that pulsed with her life blood.

"I'm here, Lyn. Waiting for you to wake up. You have a lovely daughter, sweetheart. She's just as pretty as her mother. Come on, darlin'! It's time to open those peepers.''

He was jolted out of his stupor by the clench of fingers on his.

"Michael? I really do love you, Michael."

The whisper-soft garble of words stabbed him as deeply as any spear.

"I'll still trust," he muttered, his heart aching. "No matter what, I'll trust in You. Even if the only woman I've ever loved is still in love with my brother."

Chapter Thirteen

Caitlin allowed Eliza to lift the sleeping ten-day-old baby out of her arms. She smiled at the soft looks that covered the dear faces that had gathered around to welcome them back to Wintergreen. Maryann with her daughter Amy, Beth and Veronica, Clay, Garrett, Eliza and Stan, the girls and Jordan.

But when her gaze came to the baby, her gaze stopped there, her heart pounding at the love that swelled within. She was so tiny, so delicate, such a miracle. And her own mother hadn't been awake to witness her arrival.

She clenched her teeth, holding the smile in place with difficulty.

"She's such a darling, Caitlin. I can't believe she's finally here!" Robyn brushed a finger over the soft bloom of the baby's cheek. "And so big! It's a good thing you didn't have to push her out, Caitlin."

Caitlin smiled. "Yes, isn't it just?" She refused to

look at Jordan where he stood, leaning against the
doorjamb of the living room.

"Are you feeling all right?" Olivia fluttered around
her, bringing a pillow and a cover to make her more
comfortable. "Is the incision still bothering you?"

"Not as much. It's been a while now and I'm feeling much better. It's nice to be home." That was a
lie. She felt worse than she had in months, but it
would pass. Anyway, what did it matter now that Micah was here?

"That's good. Well, come on everyone. Let's leave
the little mother to rest, now that the baby's asleep."

They filed out, one after the other, pressing a kiss
to her cheek before they left.

"Thanks for coming. I appreciate everything
you've done." Caitlin smiled until they left, then
sagged into her chair, relieved that she didn't have to
pretend anymore.

"You're in pain. Here." Jordan handed her a white
tablet and glass of water. "You can keep on ignoring
me all you like, Lyn, but I'm not going anywhere. I
promised."

"For the tenth time, I'm releasing you from that
promise. I should never have asked it of you."

"I didn't make the promise to you, I made it to
Micah right after she was born. And I'm not taking
it back. Not ever. You can be as angry as you want,
Caitlin, but I'd do the same thing again tomorrow."

She watched as he set the tumbler and pill down
on the table and ensconced himself in her armchair.

The anger, all the frustration welled up inside and she couldn't control the bitter words that poured out.

"I know, Jordan. And believe me, I'm grateful. That's what makes it so awful. It's just..." She gulped down the tears that clogged her throat. "I wanted to deliver Micah myself."

He got up, crossed the room and squatted at her feet. "I'm sorry, sweetheart. I know you're unhappy that you weren't awake when she was born. It doesn't mean anything, though. God still gave you a healthy little girl. She came through with flying colors. And you're getting better by the day. Can't you be happy about that?"

His hands closed around hers, warm and comforting and Caitlin felt overwhelmed with guilt. Why did she continue to harangue him when she knew it had to be that way?

That question was closely followed by a harder one.

Why did it always have to be that way? Why couldn't anything go according to the way she planned?

"You trusted Him, just a little, and He came through for you. Micah is the richest blessing He could have given you."

"I know." She kept her head bent, trying to ignore the wash of feelings that flowed through her every time she saw Jordan hold her daughter. "And I love her. She's so beautiful. She's so fragile! I'm just a little emotional lately."

He was as tender as any father could be, quieting

her cries, singing her songs, even changing her diaper. His love for the baby shone through in everything he did, including the small kindnesses he showered on her mother.

"I haven't thanked you for the flowers yet," she murmured, with a glance at the gorgeous red roses that overflowed her crystal vase. "You didn't have to do that."

"Yes, I did." He grinned, seating himself carefully on the cushions beside her. "I love you. And I'm proud of you. God has blessed me with the two most beautiful women in the world and I just had to share the joy." He pressed a kiss against her forehead.

"Look at that little miracle and tell me you're glad you had that operation. Caitlin. Please? There wasn't anything else we could have done."

The doctor had said the same thing the day she'd left the hospital. And Micah was a delight. Maybe it was time to let go of her anger, to give him a chance. After all, he'd stuck with her through everything. She'd been so ungrateful and he'd done so much. Why did she have to hide her feelings?

"I don't like being railroaded, Jordan. If you're going to stay in our lives, you have to stop being so pushy. I told you I didn't want milk and yet you still keep pouring me a glass. Those kinds of things do not make you likable." She smiled to show she was teasing.

"I'm already likable," he quipped, pressing a quick kiss to her lips. "It's just taking you longer to see it."

She pinched his arm.

"All right!" He held up both hands. "If you don't want milk, fine. No big deal. How do you feel about pudding?"

"Jordan!" Caitlin glared at him, but was unable to stop the corner of her mouth from turning up at his obvious caring. But then, that was the problem.

Jordan cared for her. In fact, he loved her. He'd told her far too many times for her to ignore it anymore. And Caitlin didn't know what to do about it. Here she was, mother to his brother's child, and he was acting as if he were the father. The whole situation was so confusing.

What do I feel? she asked herself for the twentieth time. What do I really feel deep down inside?

The answer wasn't easy, of course. Frustration and excitement, anger and thanksgiving, tiredness and exhilaration, pain and pleasure, happy yet sad. Everything. And nothing.

It was all mixed-up, confused. But she had Micah. That made up for all of it.

Did that mean God had answered her prayers? Or was this some sort of test?

"You're very beautiful, did you know that?" Jordan trailed a finger down the length of her nose. "Your skin glows and you look positively radiant."

"I look like I just gave birth to an eight-pound baby girl," Caitlin snorted. "And you can't keep changing the subject. You have to stop hovering, Jordan. We're fine."

"I know." He smiled tenderly. "But I like hovering, as you call it. Especially when it's over my two favorite women. So, now that the baby's here, can we talk about getting married?''

Caitlin gulped.

''I know you're tired and there are a hundred things going through your mind. My sister explained ad nauseam about hormones.'' He made a face, his mouth tipping downward in disgust.

''She did? Robyn?'' Caitlin frowned at his nod. ''What did she say?''

''Oh, a bunch of stuff about women who had C-sections feeling guilty because they didn't have a normal delivery. I told her she was crazy.'' He reached out and touched the baby's arm. ''As if there's anything to feel guilty about. This little girl is a miracle.''

''Yes, I'm beginning to realize that.'' Caitlin stared at the child who had come from her body. The thought of it stunned her. The perfectly shaped lips, the elegantly long fingers, the deep blue eyes. Micah was a miracle. And Jordan had helped get her here. She peered at him through her lashes.

''The thing is, I don't want to waste that miracle. I love you, Lyn. I want to marry you and take care of you and Micah. Couldn't we at least plan a date?''

She forced her attention away from him to stare at her fingers.

''Jordan, I've told you. I don't think I can marry you. Not now.'' *Maybe not ever,* she added silently.

''Sure you can. Doesn't have to be a big wedding, though I'd like to show you off to everyone. We could have the ceremony right here, if you want.''

His eyes shone down on her expectantly. "What do you say?"

"Jordan, I, uh, that is...the truth is, I'm not sure. I mean, everything seems so unreal to me. Everything is moving so fast. I just became a mother and now you're asking me to marry you. It's impossible to deal with!"

"Why?" His eyes narrowed, their golden lights piercing. "Are you going to say you don't love me? Because you do, Lyn. I've seen it in your eyes." His voice was so fervent she half wondered if he wasn't trying to convince himself.

"You've been really wonderful to us, coming round day after day, helping with the baby, taking care of things. And I appreciate it, Jordan. But..." Her voice trailed away as she searched for the words to express her confused feelings.

"You love me. You can't deny it. It's been there for a long time now. It's time you admit it, Lyn."

"I do like you, Jordan."

"Love," he insisted, his mouth tightening.

"I like the way you care for us, the way you make me feel loved and protected. But to get married? I don't think so, Jordan. Not yet, anyway."

"When then?"

"I don't know. Don't you see?" She was losing her focus and that was dangerous with those tiger eyes watching. "I feel like I'm only just getting back control of my life. Coming out of the anesthetic was like being back in that car, clawing my way to safety." She shuddered at the memory. "I felt like I was at

the mercy of everybody while I recovered and I hated
it.''

His eyes demanded total honesty, and Caitlin acknowledged that she owed him that.

"If I let myself get involved with you, I lose that
control again. I don't think I'm ready to do that just
yet.'' She flinched as his jaw tightened.

"We are already *involved*," he said, lurching to his
feet. "That's what love is all about.'' He glared into
the fireplace as if he wanted to tear it apart.

"And now we get to the heart of the issue. Control.
But what you really mean is that you want to go it
alone, prove to the world that you can stand out there
and take whatever it is that life deals you."

He turned around, his eyes blazing. "Why, Caitlin?
Why is it so important for you to be strong and independent, even at the risk of refusing help for your
unborn baby?''

"I didn't," she gasped, furious that he would dare
to mention that now.

"Yes, you did. And I don't think it has anything
to do with fear, Lyn. It's really all about anger, isn't
it? You're furious at all the people you love who go
away when you need them most. So you back away
from love, hide out, protect yourself. That way no one
can ever hurt you again."

"I don't do that." But she couldn't look at him,
his words cut too deep. Was she really like that? Selfish and self-centered?

"Yes, you do, Lyn. And it hurts. I think you're

trying to prove you don't need us.'' He sighed, raking a hand through his hair.

"Michael didn't *want* to die, Caitlin. Neither did your parents or your aunt. They didn't *want* to abandon you. It wasn't their fault that God called them home.'' He stopped, watching her face.

Caitlin shook her head, all the while his words raced through it. Was it true? Was she angry with all of them? Was she trying to get even in some strange way?

"You're just jealous because I chose Michael,'' she lashed out, and then wished she hadn't. Jordan was moving closer, so close she feared he wouldn't let her hide any more.

He smiled tenderly, his hands gentle as they closed around her arms.

"I know you loved my brother, Caitlin. I've accepted that. You've just had his baby. That's wonderful. Nobody could be happier than me.'' He brushed a thumb over her blouse-covered arm, fingering the warm flannel.

"But he's gone now, honey. And you love me. There's nothing wrong with that. Love isn't meant to be hoarded, it's meant to be shared. It can grow and grow.''

He wrapped his arms around her and hugged her close, his voice soothing.

"For a long time I fought against the idea of loving you, even though I knew it was true. I thought it was disloyal to Michael. You were his wife, you chose him over me. I realized almost immediately that I'd been wrong to let you go back then, you know. I had to get away from here.'' He brushed his chin against her cheek.

"When I came home, after you were married, I realized that I loved you more than ever. But you weren't mine. Still, you were very happy. I could see that. I decided that I would go away again and that I would wait. I knew the love I had for you wouldn't die. I thought I'd see what God intended for me to do with it." His hands brushed down her back.

"But sweetheart, that love didn't go away and Michael did die. He didn't want to, but he's gone. And it isn't your fault. You can't make yourself pay for his death, or your parents'. That was part of your life. A hard part, sure. But you got through it." He leaned back, his generous mouth tipped down in a frown.

"You need to accept the past and move on, Lyn. You can't make anything better by hanging on to your anger. Let it go."

Jordan's eyes glowed with an inner light that made his words all the more tenable.

"You're not a child anymore, you know that God directs our paths. You've grown up. You don't have to hide away anymore, like a scared little girl who needs protecting. You don't have to prove you can handle life. You've done that. Now you can get on with your life, because you know that He'll be there, watching out for you."

His words hit a nerve. Caitlin felt the frustration rise inside her brain, red-hot and boiling. What did he really understand? The long lonely nights when the house creaked and moaned, the reminders that she had no one of her own, the longing she felt to let go of it all and be someone completely different? Someone not quite so pathetic?

Jordan Andrews thought that he knew everything about her, that he could direct her to do his bidding no matter what she wanted. Whatever he said was law! What did he know about her worries, her fears?

"You know nothing!"

"I know more than you want me to. I know you're letting the past control the future. Our future. But I won't let you ignore our relationship. I won't."

She shoved him away, walked over to the door and yanked it open.

"You think you've got me pegged, don't you, Jordan? You think it's so easy to just toss it all away, to forget about my parents dying so horribly while I lived and watched it, to see Aunt Lucy every day and know I didn't matter to her, to pretend Michael's death didn't affect me?"

She dashed the tears away, drawing on the facade that had seen her through years of going it alone.

"I'm strong because I learned that everything comes with a price. It just depends on how much you're willing to pay."

"I know all of that affected you, Lyn. It colored the past and altered your perceptions. But now it's getting in the way of your life today."

"Thank you, Dr. Freud! Why would you even think that I could love somebody who's so hard? Michael was your brother!"

"I know that." He stood before her, his shoulders straight, his eyes shadowed. "And I loved him. But I can't live in the past, Lyn. Neither can you. I love you. I want to move on with our lives. I want all of the things God promised us."

He slipped his hand over the shining fall of curls that tumbled down her back. His touch was so delicate, so tender, Caitlin almost leaned into it.

But fear, her constant companion for years, held her back, restrained by her whispering *what ifs* inside her brain.

"I'm waiting for you, Caitlin. My family is waiting for you. We want you to join the living. They don't care that you locked them out of your life for so long. They're ready to welcome you back with open arms." Jordan swallowed. His hands dropped to his sides and his head tilted back.

Caitlin shivered, knowing something monumental would come out of those soft lips. She steeled herself.

"If your life isn't full and happy today, Caitlin, the only person you can blame is yourself. We're here, all of us. We want to love you. But you have to let us in. You can't keep withdrawing. You have to choose what you want, sweetheart. Fear, anger or love?"

Caitlin swallowed. There were tears at the corners of his eyes. His voice was sad, filled with regret.

"I can't come back, Lyn. Not until you're ready to face life and deal with its possibility of hurt. None of us controls life, that's up to God. But if we don't accept the pain, we miss the pleasure." He wrapped his arms around her and held her close to his heart, his lips against her ear.

"I love you and Micah so much. I want us to be a family, to grow together. I want to share your pain, your fears, your joys. I want to laugh with you and grieve with you. But you have to want it, too. It's time to grow up, Lyn. It's time to choose. What will it be? Love? Or safety by yourself in your shell of self-pity?"

Jordan kissed her so tenderly Caitlin thought she'd melt. She could have stayed there forever, but mere seconds later his arms fell away.

His lips touched hers one last time, his voice aching in its intensity. When he looked at her, she could feel the love in his eyes reaching out, desperately trying to touch her frozen heart.

"Choose love, Caitlin. Please, choose me."

And then he was gone.

Chapter Fourteen

"Choose me."

Caitlin shook herself out of the fog Jordan had left her in.

She closed the door, entered her apartment and started up the stairs, determined to get on with her life. She was a single mother, alone, with a baby. She had responsibilities. She had to be strong.

The sound of brakes applied too heavily rang through the house. Caitlin stopped, her eyes wide with fear. Jordan! Was he hurt?

"Not again! Please God, not again! I can't lose Jordan, too. I love him so much."

The knowledge coursed through her like a lightning bolt, awakening her to the folly of letting him go.

She'd let him walk out the door without telling him how much she loved him. Not the same as she'd loved Michael, it was true. This love was different.

But it was a deep and lasting love that would be a foundation for the future.

Caitlin raced for the front door, ripped it open and stood on tiptoes, staring to the west as her heart beat double time. What was the pain of the past compared to the grief she now felt, knowing she'd turned him away, knowing she loved him more than life.

Relief swamped her as she spied his car, patiently waiting at the end of the block for a young boy to cross the intersection.

Jordan, dear Jordan. He was fine. He was alive!

Caitlin sank down onto the thickly braided rug inside the front door of Wintergreen, her mind whirling with the wonder of it.

She loved Jordan Andrews. Loved him. With all her heart and soul and mind. Of course, she had loved Michael, too; but that was a different kind of love. She'd been young and needy. She'd expected Michael to care for her, to protect her, to cherish her. She'd never even considered what her young husband might need from her, and never found out how their marriage would have worked, what she would have contributed to their union.

But she had to consider it now. Jordan was here, alive and well, and in love with her. He didn't want a little girl for a wife, he wanted a woman who was prepared to stand by his side and face the world head-on, good or bad.

"He needs me to be there for him," she murmured, trying to sort it all out. "He wants me to share his life."

But to share meant giving herself, freely, without holding back. Could she do that? Anything less would be cheating, a childish pretense that would hurt him. And she and Micah would suffer as much as Jordan. They needed him in their lives, needed his comfort, his compassion, his strength.

But most of all they needed his love, backing them, supporting them as they supported him. There would be problems, certainly. But, oh, the joy she'd share. How wonderful it would be to just let go and love him.

Jordan was gone.

He wouldn't come back. Not now. Not when she'd turned him away, mocked him for pointing out how childish she had been. He'd given her the chance, asked her to trust him, and she'd turned him away, let him walk out of her life and Micah's.

Bleakly she watched the taillights of his car disappear.

Caitlin pushed the door closed, then burst into tears at the enormity of what she'd done. Jordan had left believing that she didn't want him, didn't need his arms around her, his lips close to hers. How could she have denied herself the one thing she most wanted?

"Caitlin? Caitlin, what in the world is wrong?" Maryann stood inside, staring. After a moment she hunched down beside her, tugging at her shoulder. "Is it the baby?"

"Why doesn't she answer? What's wrong with

her?'' Beth's concerned voice only encouraged her tears and Caitlin sobbed all the harder.

"I forgot to tell you... What in the world is going on here?'' Eliza's worried voice broke through the others' conversation. She listened to the others for a moment, then tugged on Caitlin's arm.

"Tell me what's wrong?'' she encouraged, a tiny smile twitching at the corner of her lips.

"She keeps asking for Jordan.''

"Ah! I thought so. Come on, dear. Inside before you catch your death.'' They urged her to the sofa. "Spill it all,'' Eliza ordered.

"I've ruined everything,'' Caitlin sobbed after the whole story had poured out. "He'll think I only want him here for Micah if I tell him I love him now. He'll think I can't stand on my own two feet!''

"Good gracious. I've never seen you so out of control. Mop up, my girl. We've got work to do. I haven't coaxed and coached things this far to let everything fall apart now.''

Eliza motioned to Beth and Maryann and Caitlin watched as they formed a circle in the middle of the room.

"What are you talking about?'' she asked uncertainly. There was something in Eliza's glance that sent a squiggle of reservation up her spine.

"We're talking about your future, my dear. A wonderful happy future that you deserve and that I intend to see that you have.'' She smiled. "You don't think I'm going to throw all my hard work away, do you? No sir!''

Caitlin thought she looked like a cat that had lunched on a canary and now just finished a very big bowl of thick cream.

"Now go with Maryann, my dear. She'll help you change. Beth and I have things to do. First of all we need flowers. Lots of flowers."

"What things? Why do I need to change?" Caitlin dashed the tears from her eyes, frowning at them all. "What are you doing?"

"Playing Fairy Godmother," Eliza giggled as she brushed a stack of baby clothes into Maryann's arms and waved her arm toward the stairs. "It's my best role."

Caitlin flinched, stunned by the glow of anticipation in those eyes that were so like her baby's.

"Come on, Caitlin. Let's get you pretty."

Caitlin trailed Maryann up the stairs, her forehead creased. "What are they doing?"

"Planning a nice romantic dinner for you and Jordan. And it's about time!"

Two hours after he'd left Lyn's, Jordan was headed back. He kept his foot pressed to the floor, ignoring the yellow lights and honking horns. Caitlin needed him his mother said. There was no time to dillydally. This was important.

He made the corner to her cul-de-sac on two wheels, barely missing a station wagon that was illegally parked by a hydrant.

"Calm down," he ordered his racing heart. "Everything's fine. The baby's not sick, Lyn's okay. Mom would have said if it was serious. Take a deep breath. You're not a kid going out on his first date!"

It didn't help much. He still lurched to a stop in front of the old Victorian house with a squeal that would have done a teenager proud.

"Probably burst a pipe in this mausoleum," he consoled himself as he loped up the walkway and took the stairs three at a time. "Or the furnace went out. Yeah, that's probably it. The furnace."

He punched her doorbell four times in rapid succession before he could physically force his hand down. The door was oak and really solid, but he figured if she didn't answer in about twenty seconds, he would kick it in.

The door opened.

"Hi." Lyn, his Lyn, stood there smiling, her hair gleaming as it flowed over her shoulders in a river of curls. She wore a dress in some green velvet stuff that showed she hadn't kept so much as an ounce of Micah's baby fat. If she had, it was well placed. "Come on in."

Jordan stepped through the door, puzzled by her calm demeanor and elegant dress. Surely that oaf Matthews wasn't going to show up again?

"Uh, Mom said you needed me?" He let her take his coat, then followed meekly when she led the way into her apartment.

"Yes. Yes, Jordan I do."

Inside the door, he stopped short and stared. There were candles everywhere, flickering on the soft light of late afternoon. A fire glowed in the hearth, flowers bloomed on the mantel. To Jordan it looked like home.

"Come on in. Dinner's ready whenever we are." She smiled at him and he got lost in that look. Her eyes glowed with something warm and exciting. What was it?

Jordan swallowed when she turned around, and followed her, trailing behind, through to the dining room.

"Have a seat."

He stayed where he was, his eyes fixed on the gorgeous bouquet of red roses sitting in the middle of a table prepared for an intimate dinner for two. He looked at her again. She was smiling that smile again. His palms started to sweat. Something told him this wasn't a dress rehearsal for Clay.

"Uh, Caitlin?"

"Yes?" She stood there, waiting, her hands clasped together in front of her.

"What exactly is this about?"

She smiled. It started in her eyes, but the effect was transported across her entire face.

"I just thought you might like to enjoy a nice romantic dinner before I ask you to marry me."

Jordan gulped. He couldn't move, couldn't look away from her. His whole body was on full alert. Was she serious? It was too good to be true, wasn't it?

Then he saw her fingers knot together and knew that she was just as nervous as he. That unlocked the block of his chest. He walked over to where she stood and took her hands in his, warming their icy coldness with his warmth.

"*You're* going to ask *me* to marry *you?*"

She nodded. "Mmm-hmm."

"Why?"

"Because I love you. I have for a long time. I've tried to run from it, pretend it isn't there, blame it on

Micah. I can't do it anymore. I'm too old to play games. I don't even want to.''

"What do you want?'' He didn't know how he got the words out of his mouth, his heart was beating so fast.

"I want to be your wife, to live with you, to share your dreams. I don't want to run away anymore, Jordan.''

He pulled her into his arms, prepared to forgive anything as long as she loved him.

She tugged back. "Wait a minute, Jordan. I have to say this first.''

"It doesn't matter, Lyn. None of it. I love you, you love me. That's what counts. And Micah, of course.'' He grinned, ecstatic that he wouldn't miss any time away from the little girl.

"It does matter, Jordan. Micah is Michael's daughter. I can't change that. I don't want to.'' She took a deep breath and continued.

Jordan watched the flicker of candlelight on her face and wondered uncertainly if they would ever get past Michael and find their own place.

"When I married Michael, I was a child. A girl who was so afraid of life that she grabbed on to the first anchor she found. I loved him without knowing what love meant and he was gone before I could find out.'' She searched his face, eyes dark with worry. "Do you understand?''

He nodded.

"When you came back, I realized that I didn't really know anything about love. Michael was the giver, I was the taker.''

"He wanted it that way, Lyn. Michael loved you.''

"I know." She sighed, unshed tears making her jade eyes glisten. "But I've grown up now, Jordan. I've learned that God is the only shield I need against trouble. He'll always be there, no matter what. I can face anything with you. Anything."

"I love you," he whispered. Then he kissed her as he'd longed to do so many years ago, just last week, early one morning when he'd visited her at the hospital and found she was coming home.

"I love you so much."

She relaxed against him, her fingers twining about his neck. He would have kissed her again, long and satisfyingly, except that she tilted her head back and raised one eyebrow.

"What?" He was half-afraid to ask.

"Well, I was just wondering if this means you'll marry me. Please? Forever. As long as we both shall live."

A sparkle in her eyes told him she already knew the answer, so he pretended to prevaricate.

"Hmm. I'll have to think about it. Does Micah come as part of the deal? She's already my daughter in here." He tapped his chest.

She frowned. "Of course!"

"And will you promise to love, honor and *obey* me?" He burst out laughing at the dour look on her face.

"You're pushing it, Jordan! I meant for this to be a happy evening. I mean, I have the ring and everything." She pulled the black box out of her pocket.

"Oh, you got me an engagement ring?" He flipped the lid open and lifted out the ring he'd chosen weeks ago, shaking his head as he turned the ring from side to side. Its facets shimmered and shone in the candlelight.

"I have to tell you, Lyn, this is a little gaudy for me."

She held out her left hand and slipped her finger inside the ring before he could move.

"I'll just look after it for you then, shall I?" Her eyes sparkled up at him.

"For how long?" he demanded, replacing his arm around her waist.

"Forever," she promised, sealing the deal with a kiss.

A long time later Jordan glanced at his ring on her finger.

"I have to tell you, I don't think this is such a good deal," he complained, snuggling her head against his shoulder as they both watched the baby sleep.

"Why?" She stared at her hand, twisting her finger this way and that in the moonlight. "I think it's a great deal."

"What do I get as a reminder of your promise of love?" he demanded. "How do I know that you won't run away the first time I muddy the kitchen floor or forget to wash the porridge pot?"

"You never mentioned porridge." Caitlin frowned.

"I didn't?" He brushed a knuckle down her nose. "I love porridge. Especially if it's a day old or so."

She reached up to stroke one hand across his chin.

"I'll tell you what. The day we're married, I'll give you my promise embedded in gold and fixed on your finger for life. As long as you promise to wash the pot when you're finished."

He pretended to consider it.

"I guess that would be okay. When and where are we getting married?"

"At Wintergreen, of course!" She looked scandalized that he hadn't thought of it. "After all, it's only fitting that the Widow of Wintergreen renounce her status as an independent, self-reliant woman. And when else would we get married but at Thanksgiving."

He nodded, liking the idea more and more.

"The garden will be buried in snow, of course, but we could have everything in here. That way, we'll be well and truly married before Christmas."

"Why's that so important?" He blinked at the glitter of mischief in her eyes.

"Because I've got the perfect thing to go into your stocking. So what do you think?"

He must have liked the idea. Jordan was too busy kissing her to reply.

Epilogue

"**I** can't believe I let you talk Caitlin into this."
Jordan glared at his mother with a look that wasn't
totally pretend.

"All this falderal when all we wanted was to get
married. Look at me! I look like a turkey."

"You can say that again." Robyn grinned as she
straddled Eudora on her hip. "Smile!" She snapped
yet another picture, giggling at his threatening look.
"I love it."

"Mother!" Jordan clenched his fists to stop himself
from strangling them both. "Can't you do something?"

"Of course I can. Go away now, Robyn, dear. I
have to get your brother calm so he won't forget his
vows. I want everything to be nice for Caitlin."

"We wanted Thanksgiving you know," he sputtered, shoving the huge poinsettia out of his way.
"We were going to have a small ceremony. A *private*
ceremony."

"How ridiculous! I'm glad I was able to help her see the light. Now bend down, Jordan. Your bow tie is crooked." When he didn't obey immediately, she pinched his arm. "I don't know why you men fuss so much. It's only a wedding, after all."

Jordan rolled his eyes, but controlled the groan. She wouldn't thank him for pointing out the ruckus she'd created over the wedding cake, nor the fact that she'd ordered more flowers than three weddings required.

"Caitlin's home, *our* home," he corrected himself, "looks like a garden."

"Do you think so, dear? Oh, thank you." She hugged him tight and then bustled out of the room. "Try not to get dirty, Jordan. And stay put. I have to go help Caitlin."

Jordan grinned and then checked his watch for the umpteenth time that morning. Six more minutes. Then they could get on with this production and he'd be one step closer to being married. He fell into thought dreaming about that.

"Good grief, Jordan!" Robyn shook her head in disbelief. "The whole place is waiting for the groom to come out. Caitlin thinks you've changed your mind. What's the problem?"

"Robyn, you're a wonderful wife and I'm truly glad that you love me as much you do. And I thank God every day that you're not afraid to stand up for what you believe. But right now darling, and I mean this in the nicest possible way, go away." Her husband gently eased her out the door and smiled as she stomped away.

"I told you I can take care of my wife." He winked at Jordan. "Ready, big guy?"

"Yes," Jordan sighed happily. "More than ready."

He sucked in his breath when Caitlin moved slowly down the stairs. Her suit was the palest pink, the short trim jacket giving way to a long straight skirt with a scalloped hem. She held dark-pink roses and lilies. A fluffy little veil sat perched on her head.

To him she was the most beautiful sight in the world as his father led her down an aisle formed between rows of chairs and up to the area circled by dark pink poinsettias, where he stood with their minister.

"You're late," he whispered, taking her hand.

"So were you." She smiled and the tension left him. This was right, this was good, this was blessed.

"'Old things are gone. Behold, all things are as new.'" The minister's words rang around the room like the bells on Christmas morning.

"I now pronounce you husband and wife. You may kiss the bride."

From her grandmother's arms, Micah mewled a tiny cry, then shoved her fist in her mouth. Seconds later her lashes flopped closed and she slept, a furtive smile curving the corners of her bow-shaped mouth as her parents celebrated their love.

* * * * *

Don't miss the next book in
Lois Richer's BRIDES OF THE SEASONS
series, DADDY ON THE WAY,
coming in November from Love Inspired.

Dear Reader,

I hope you've enjoyed *Baby on the Way*. I've learned so much from writing Caitlin's story. Have you ever had one of those weeks when nothing seems to go right? Or maybe it's lasted months, or years! It's hard during those times to remember that God loves us more than we can ever know or understand. Isn't it amazing that in spite of our frustration and anger and worry, He can make something beautiful out of us, if we'll just allow Him to work?

My hope is that you will find the silver lining in every cloud that God sends your way. I wish you peace and joy, but above all, I wish you abundant, restoring love in every moment of your life.